D1524000

ANTHONY'S STORY

the KILL SQUAD

WINSTON LEGGE

Author of: Knots in the Vine, Indictment of Johnson County, and Benson's Plan

CHAPTER ONE

HELLO! My name is Anthony Moretti. This is the story of my life. As you may have thought when reading my name, I am of Italian descent.

I was born in the "Real Little Italy" section of the Bronx Borough of New York City. My given name was derived from that of my deceased Grandfather. My Grandparents had immigrated from Italy to seek work and a better life. They located, along with many other Italian immigrants, in Saint Louis, Missouri, where jobs were available in plants making bricks.

These Italians mostly settled in an area that became known as "Dago Hill". In years after, in the dawn of "political correctness", the Italian slur was removed and the area became "the Hill". Nothing, however, could take away the song composed in 1926 with the title "Dago Hill Blues", popular to the present in Saint Louis.

The Hill is now a local and tourist attraction famous for many wonderful true Italian restaurants.

Two well-known baseball players, Yogi Berra and Joe Garagiola, were products of the Hill. While Yogi had a Hall of Fame baseball career, he may be best remembered for his takeoff of the saying "the opera is not over until the fat lady sings" when he coined "it ain't over until it's over".

My father left Saint Louis when he became just old enough to join the United States Army during World War II. After his military service, which he extended for a few years, his decision was against going home to find work, most likely in the restaurant business. Lured by the bright lights of the biggest city, he moved to the Bronx. Ironically, the employment he found was with a Bronx Italian restaurant. A co-worker was a very attractive young girl, also of Italian heritage, who was a New York city native.

There was a short romance and engagement, followed by a Catholic wedding, with only immediate family, due to very little money being available. Because both had only minimum income employment, their choice was to wait several years to have children. By the time I was born, my parents had purchased a small grocery store on Arthur Avenue.

We lived in a two bedroom, two bath apartment just one block off of Arthur Avenue. It was only two years after my birth that my sister, Anna, followed. We were always close. She was, and remained, my best friend for life. During the many difficult situations one finds during childhood, we were always there for each other, consoling, comforting, or defending. We could talk about anything, no matter how personal, such as educational, social, sexual or family matters.

When we were old enough for separate bedrooms, Anna kept the actual bedroom, while I had a single bed that would just fit into a large closet. We shared the bathroom. I do not recall any argument about usage time.

In my early years, I would wonder why we did not move to a larger home. As I became older, I understood that my parents eked out a living with little money left over. I learned as a teenager that New York had rent control laws that prohibited landlords from increasing rents above legally established amounts. This was designed to keep lower income families in their homes. We were lower income.

An automobile was out of the question, both for the vehicle original cost and the prohibitive cost of parking. The rare trips to Manhattan were about fifteen minutes by subway, and in the Bronx we walked.

I can vividly recall my eighth birthday. On a Sunday, my father took me to a New York Yankees baseball game. Most every male child in the Bronx is a Yankee fan, and I was thrilled. Our tickets were in the least expensive section of the outfield. I was told beforehand that I could buy only one soft drink and one hotdog. None of this mattered. I was a kid at a baseball game in Yankee Stadium.

Our clothes were purchased at discount and second-hand stores, except that our mother sewed prom and dance dresses for my sister. This was not a problem as most of the kids at our schools were in the same financial circumstances. When I reached teenage dance age, a second-hand suit was purchased that did not fit perfectly. I did not go to many of the dances, but the suit was my usual attire for Sunday Church. We attended Our Lady of Mount Carmel Catholic Church. Anna and I were required to be there, no excuses.

My parents were avid bridge and penny poker players. There was a couple in the neighborhood that came over on regular nights to play one or the other of these games. I was taught a little of the bridge game and would often be called to play a hand or two when a bathroom break was needed. While bridge required four participants, two pairs of partners, poker could be played by more. I was occasionally allowed to play if I had enough pennies. I did not like bridge as it was a partnership game requiring coordination with another person. Poker, I loved, as each player could make decisions and plays based upon his/her sole judgment. You will learn later that poker played an important role in my adult life.

By my second year in high school, I had reached my full height of five feet, ten inches, with a stocky build of one hundred ninety pounds. The school coaches encouraged me to play football. I was big enough and rather athletic.

As I think back on my life, I was more a loner than team player. I selected to decline football, but found my passion in the sport of boxing. My school did not have a team, but New York was noted for amateur boxing. There was a gym within walking distance that would allow young boys with talent to train without charge. The trainers were paid by professional boxers, but would work with promising amateurs when they had time. I received a lot of help and soon moved into real matches in the New York area.

As might have been expected, I spent more and more time boxing at the expense of school work. I sometimes skipped school to go to the gym. In only fifteen months, I was the top rated boxer in my weight class in New York City. I had only nine matches under my belt, but had won all by knockout in the first or second rounds.

In the same time frame, I almost failed my high school grade. I had to go to summer school to advance. My parents ended my boxing career, over my protests, as they were strong in their desire that I should have the education they missed.

CHAPTER TWO

Socially, Anna was among the most popular in our high school and church. She was beautiful and outgoing, very smart, but never one to assume she was special. I was much more the quiet one. While there were a few boys I considered friends, I never had the best friend that was common in our age group.

This was long after the so-called "sexual revolution". Anna and I both, as teenagers, were sexually active. Anna, however, was unlikely to have sex during the first two or three dates with a boy, while I focused on the girls that had a reputation for first date sex.

Actually, I never had a steady girlfriend during my teenage years. There were two or three girls I liked better than others, but nothing worked out for a long-term relationship. Looking back, I can blame myself for not making better efforts at conversation and seeking mutual interests.

The Bronx was, and still is, noted for the highest

rate of teen pregnancy in New York City. A lot was due to ignorance, but probably more to lack of preparation. A girl generally expected the boy to have and use a condom. In a passionate situation, where the boy was not prepared, it was difficult for the girl to stop at the point just before penetration. Many times the couple did not stop and just hoped pregnancy would not happen. Too often, it did.

My sister would tease me by saying "if you don't have a cover, keep it in your pants".

Anna had been dating a boy for about two weeks. He went to our church, was considered a good student, and played on our high school football team. She seemed to like him more than a lot of her other dates. One Saturday night, she came home later than usual with a bruise on her face. When I inquired, she broke into tears before telling me of her ordeal.

The relationship had developed to a point where she was willing to have sex, actually looking forward to expanding the relationship. They reached a heated moment when she discovered he was not prepared with a condom. He wanted to continue and a strong argument ensued. She refused to give in. He went into a rage before hitting her.

She asked me not to go after him. While agreeing they would not date again, my typically nice, sweet Anna, felt she knew sex was on the horizon. She then blamed herself for not putting a condom in her purse.

It was a rarity that I did not follow any request by my sister, but her bruised face made this an exception. After school on Monday, I called him out and proceeded to administer a severe beating. He looked so bad that the parents took their son to a hospital emergency room to be checked. Their complaint to the school administration got me a one-week suspension. My parents were upset, Anna felt bad, but I was content with myself.

CHAPTER THREE

Segregation by race or skin color is not part of life in the Bronx. However, segregation by wealth/income is clear throughout the Borough. Try to compare wealthy Riverdale and Throggs Neck neighborhoods to the poverty of the South Bronx, and you will find there is no comparison. The wealthy live apart and safe from the poor, crime-infested neighborhoods. Such is the way it was when I was growing up. Little has changed over the years.

The Bronx is known for Yankee Stadium, the Bronx Zoo, the Botanical Gardens, and the Italian restaurants and shops of the area called Arthur Avenue, Belmont or Little Italy of the Bronx. The latter is where my parents had their grocery, with our home nearby.

Visitors ask if the Bronx is safe. Certainly, there are safe areas (or generally safe), but overall the Bronx, especially the South Bronx, can be very dangerous.

In the eighteen years I lived at home with my parents and sister, the South Bronx was noted for the most violent crime in the city. The 1970's were super bad and dangerous. Nothing changed a lot over the years, although city and law enforcement officials began about 1990 to cite figures showing drops in some types of crime.

The unsolvable problem is the huge amount of poverty. The last figures I saw had the poverty rate for the entire Borough at thirty percent, making the Bronx the poorest Borough of the five comprising New York City. The annual income of our residents is not even half of the Upper East Side, and the gap seems to increase with time.

The population is the youngest in our city, about thirty-five percent black, and a majority of Hispanics, primarily from Puerto Rico, when black Hispanics are included. Many have moved to the city without money, education, or job skills, often speaking only Spanish. They live in public housing, subsisting on welfare and other government programs. Crime is rampant, much gang related, including drugs, robbery, theft, prostitution, assault and murder.

The Arthur Avenue area where my parents worked, and where we lived, is mostly safe. Venture a few blocks away, especially at night, and danger lurks. If you are a white tourist, you may be in for big trouble.

The more distance one walks in the Bronx, the more likely an assault will occur. Do not walk anywhere after dark. It is night when the gang bangers, the homeless, drug addicts, prostitutes, and the combinations of those come out. If you began walking around in the late evening/early morning hours, I would expect that you would be attacked and even shot.

I don't know the names of all the gangs, but one that writes its name on many buildings is the Crips. There is some gang warfare, but they are more likely looking for easy targets to prey on.

I have been asked many times to name the most dangerous area in the Borough. A subjective answer is required, as different Bronx residents would have thoughts based on their personal experiences and information. I can tell you that I would most likely start with East Tremont. If you are white, and wander there at night, I would bet you will be killed.

Hunts Point is an industrial area with a much smaller population than some others. But it is a "red light" district, frequented by whores and pimps, and has high violent crime statistics.

Following my first thoughts, I can name Morrisania, Brownsville, East NY, Decatur and Port Morris. With only very little additional thought, I could add more names. Any areas with the public housing projects will have extensive crime.

The worst pockets of crime are in the 40th, 41th, and 42nd police precincts, all located in the South Bronx. Three really bad neighbors are Morrisania, Rivera's, and Crotona Park, all in the 42nd.

The New York Police Department will point out, and I believe accurately, that total crime in the Bronx is down somewhat in recent years. However, the major crimes of rape, robbery, felony assault and grand larceny remain high when compared to the rest of the city.

I have personally experienced only one serious incident involving street crime in the Bronx. Actually, "extremely serious" might be a better

description. We will get to a full account of this in
due time.

CHAPTER FOUR

I finally graduated from high school. This was a relief as I just did not like attending classes, studying and having to take tests. I should have shown more interest, but school was simply not my thing. Receiving a diploma was satisfying. Actually, I did not know then, but the diploma was a requirement for a path I would want to take in my future.

Following graduation, I worked in my parents grocery store for a couple of months until my eighteenth birthday when I enlisted in the United States Army.

My father had dreamed of me attending college at nearby Fordham University in the Bronx. He was disappointed to some extent, but discussed with me that my high school grades were far from good enough for a scholarship, and there was no family money to pay for college. There was some potential for me to obtain a scholarship at a college that had a boxing team, but I really did not like the thought of classes and study to try to make satisfactory grades. The army was my best chance for a good life away from the Bronx.

My army career began with basic infantry
training at Fort Jackson, South Carolina. I traveled
on the subway to a train running to Washington
where I met a bus filled with recruits like me.
Everyone was far too excited to sleep on the bus
which arrived at about five o'clock in the morning.

We took our belongings to the barracks where we
would be housed, and then followed a sergeant to a
building to be issued uniforms (the standard army
green) and black boots. The dining area, called the
"mess hall", was next for breakfast. We were issued
metal trays and proceeded down a line where the
food was served onto our trays. The breakfast food
was chipped beef on toast, a gray gravy type
substance poured over the toast. I learned later this
was known in the army as "shit on a shingle". Being
really hungry, I made a mistake by asking for an
additional serving. The response to my request was
an amount poured onto my tray that would have fed
two people. Little did I know that, during basic
training, if the food was on your tray, you ate it all,
every bite. I was almost sick by the time I was
finished.

Since we had been on the bus all night, I made an assumption we would now go to quarters for some sleep. Wrong assumption! We would work all day with lights out for sleep at nine that night.

The next morning we awoke to the sound of a bugle accompanied by an army sergeant yelling "Drop your cocks and grab your socks, fall out. When I say fall out, I don't want to see anything but asses and elbows." What an introduction to nine weeks of basic combat training.

Fort Jackson in July and August has got to be one of the hottest places in our country. Basic training was rigorous. Our company commander was a recent college grad who had completed army ROTC to get his officer commission. He was a distance runner on his college track team and led us on many tiring runs through the hills and heat.

I had an advantage in physical condition from my boxing training. All of the hands-on teaching was conducted by sergeants with many years of army service. They seemed impressed with my physical condition, and even more so with my boxing reputation.

While combat basic training is required of all recruits, it is based on requirements particular to the infantry. Hand-to-hand and bayonet fighting, various weapons and explosives. This was what I wanted. I managed to excel in all areas. Praise was not a part of a sergeant's makeup, but I could tell that I likely rated first in our CBT class.

I wanted to continue into Specials Forces. There was an age requirement of twenty years, so I would have to wait to apply. In the meantime, I needed to be accepted into the infantry "Military Occupational Status", called "MOS". We all started with MOS 11x meaning "basic".

Following graduation from basic training, my hope was realized. I was assigned MOS 11b which was the infantry designation. This designation was, and remains to this day, the most honored in the United States Army. The infantry duty is defined to "close with the enemy to kill, wound or capture him".

To be eligible for Special Forces, soldiers must follow combat basic training with Advanced Individual Training and the U.S. Army Airborne School. I immediately applied and was granted acceptance to both AIT and Airborne School. I learned at this point that my high school diploma was an absolute requirement for Special Forces. I could thank my parents for staying on me about school.

CHAPTER FIVE

I had a short break between completing Basic Training and starting Advanced Individual Training, so I traveled back to the Bronx to visit with my family. All was well. My parents seemed healthy, staying busy with the grocery store, along with the social times of bridge and poker with their friends.

Anna was now a senior in high school, beautiful as always, homecoming queen, National Honor Society, and with a rank of number one scholastically in her class. A full scholarship to Fordham University was forthcoming which would complete my father's dream of having a child receive a college degree.

I was so happy to see Anna. She was always the same. With all her popularity and success, she remained unpretentious, sweet and caring.

After school, I took her to the local bar that was known to serve alcohol to anyone that walked in the door. Teenagers were a big part of the bar business. Anna did not drink much, but we had a couple of beers along with a lot of conversation. She was happy. I was happy. Our lives were moving on a good schedule.

Our mother had left the grocery early that afternoon to prepare a special dinner in Italian fashion. While the military provided ample food, it was not noted for fine preparation. Nothing I had in the past months compared to this home-cooked meal. We all laughed when I told of my experience with "shit on a shingle". My father knew exactly what I was talking about.

I spent the next morning helping at the grocery. In the afternoon, I enjoyed visiting the gym where I had learned boxing. The training staff seemed glad to see me. We discussed my army life along with military stories from those who had served. Sometimes we would spar a few rounds for fun.

On this afternoon I lost track of time at the gym. It was after dark when I began the walk home. You may recall I alluded to a "major incident – very serious" in an earlier part of my story. This is it.

Walking alone, I was approached by two black males. A few feet away, one said "white bro, give us your money." I immediately launched a right-hand punch that sent him to the sidewalk. Almost instantly, I felt a pain in my right side from a knife welded by the other male. My left hook punch left him unconscious on the concrete.

Realizing he had tried to kill me, I went into a rage, picked up the knife, and drove it deep into his chest, through his heart. I turned to do the same to the other assailant, also unconscious on the sidewalk, when I saw he was a young boy, perhaps only thirteen or fourteen years old.

My rage immediately subsided as panic set in. I had just killed someone. I headed to a nearby hospital emergency room, throwing the knife into a garbage dumpster along the way.

I had been fortunate. The knife blade had passed through my jacket, through my heavy belt, and was stopped by my hip bone. My wound was superficial, cleaned and bandaged by the hospital staff in short order. I declined to make a police report. I also lied as to the location of the assault while claiming there was only one man involved, a white man.

Back at home, my jacket covered my blood

stained shirt. I went up stairs to change shirts, placing the bloody one in my army bag. I never told my parents or sister what had happened.

On the long trip back to my duty assignment, I thought a lot about killing the man. With both assailants on the concrete, I could have safely left for the hospital without inflicting further harm. Even though I was the victim of an attempted robbery, had I committed murder by this unnecessary killing? This was the first time I had thought that the army training to kill might have impacted my personality. Time would tell.

CHAPTER SIX

Advanced Individual Training in the army was no piece of cake, just as demanding as Combat Basic Training. The biggest difference to me was that each soldier was taught and practiced in more specific detail. We were still preparing to seek and destroy an enemy.

The next step was Army Airborne School. Certainly, I had never before jumped from an airplane. The truth was I had never before been in an airplane.

The school was not long, three weeks at Fort Benning, Georgia. This was different from Advanced Individual Training, where the training time varied with your MOS. I lost track of time in AIT, but believed we were in training about six weeks.

The first week of Airborne School involved a lot of running and other physical exercise. We became familiar with the equipment, how to put on the parachute rig, took classes on jumping procedures,

24

and jumped off a platform to perfect the landing fall. Military parachutes are not like the sky diving apparatus where you see someone land softly in a standing position. You land very hard.

The last day of the first week, and at the beginning of week two, we used a zip line out of a thirty-four-foot tower. We then moved to door training (jumping through a mock airplane door), followed by emergencies such tangled chutes and landing in trees. Ending the second week, we jumped from the famous Fort Benning two-hundred-fifty foot tower.

The third and final week, we first went over all we had learned in the preceding two weeks. Then the time had arrived. I entered an airplane for the first time in my life with the knowledge that my exit would be by jumping out from a high altitude. Even with all the prior study and training, I felt I might vomit or piss in my pants.

There were five total jumps, two in full combat gear, two "Hollywood" jumps with only a main and reserve chute. And the final, a night jump also with full combat gear. After surviving the first jump, I looked forward to the remainder except for the night jump which, honestly, scared the crap out of me.

Having completed Airborne School (since I am writing you know I survived the night jump), I now had met all the requirements to take the Special Forces Preparation Course (SFPC) except I was not yet twenty years of age. I had been able to speak with the Commanding Officer for the SFPC at Fort Bragg, North Carolina. He seemed to like me and my determination to become a Special Forces Soldier. He made arrangements for me to be assigned to the army post at Vilseck, Germany until I reached birthday number twenty.

This was an easy assignment, normal work hours, and a lot of recreational time. Visiting a foreign country was an exciting new adventure for me. Upon learning I was going to Vilseck, a seasoned sergeant gave me advice from his years of service around the world.

First, I should learn to speak as much German as possible. Effort would be appreciated. Second, if I did not drink beer, learn to do so, a requirement of German life. Third, avoid the off-base bars where most of the American soldiers go. Instead, I should spend my drinking hours in the bars frequented by local Germans. Once the locals could see I was trying to speak the language and learn their customs, they could be friendly and a pleasant experience.

I would follow the old sergeant's recommendations. I bought a basic book about German language to read on the flight over. Before landing, I had mastered four words I considered critical. Bier (beer), danke (thank you), herrentoilette (men's toilet), and three ways to say taverne (die taverne; die wirtshaus; die schenke). I would soon work on the words for "hello" and "goodbye".

I quickly settled into life on the army post. My work duties seemed so easy following the rigid structure of the training I had finished. The living quarters were nice, though standard, barracks for lower-ranked enlisted like me. The food was on the excellent side for army "chow".

The first time I ventured into a German tavern, I was ignored by the customers enjoying their beer and conversation. I thought about just going to the taverns frequented by the other soldiers, but made the good decision to give the locals another try.

This time, a young couple remembered I had been there before. They both spoke some English and invited me to join their table. Over a few trips to this same tavern, and a lot of "bier", I felt like I was being included as a friend. Many spoke good English. There was obvious appreciation that I was trying to learn German. They wanted to know about life in the United States, so we had a mutual German-American interest. And we all liked German beer.

The tavern which seemed to have adopted me had a very pretty waitress, about my age, whose name was Emma. I was attracted, but assumed someone so cute and personable would have one or more boyfriends. I was not going to chance making a move on her.

One night, after several weeks, I was paying my bill to leave, when Emma asked if I was married. Explaining that she was off work on Sunday, I was invited to her home for a Sunday noon meal. Thrilled, I accepted, got directions, and waited for the weekend.

Emma lived in a small and neat home with her parents. Her older brother was away in the German army. The food her mother cooked was typically German and delicious. Emma and her parents were all fluent in English. I felt some shame that I had not learned another language during my ample time in high school. The conversation was as good as the meal.

That day started a regular Sunday date. We walked, talked, and laughed, all while becoming very close. Emma confided that she had dated numerous German young men throughout her teenage years. As would be expected, most were much more interested in sex than companionship. She was one year older than my nineteen.

After several weeks, our relationship became intense, sexual, wonderful. She was the first love in my young life. I could tell she had these same feelings about me. Emma was constantly on my mind. At the conclusion of each date, I was waiting for the days to pass for the next. Of course, I would see her at the tavern, but we had agreed not to disclose our relationship to the other patrons. She needed to work, tips were her primary income, and appearing free to flirt with young men was a source of good tips.

Time moved fast as my birthday approached. One morning I received my order to report to Fort Bragg in anticipation that I would commence SFPC as the next step toward Special Forces Qualification.

I was almost in tears. I knew this time was approaching. I had kept myself from thinking about the decision I would have to make. I could leave Emma for the Special Forces, or I could decline the assignment, stay in the regular army in Germany, and marry Emma.

I will not further detail the agony in my decision. I left Germany and Emma for Fort Bragg.

I will say I never forgot Emma, her smiling face, the hours we walked, talked, laughed and loved. I thought at the time I was choosing the Special Forces over the love of my life. It was difficult for a young man only approaching twenty years in this world to understand that first love and true love are often not the same.

It would be some years down the road before I would meet Bethany Hamilton. In this story of my life, I will try to describe a love affair with her that may be beyond my ability for description. I cannot

give a definition of true love. I can say that, if you
continue to read, you will meet Bethany and
understand how the relationship we have can be
condensed into the two words – true love!

CHAPTER SEVEN

Arriving at Fort Bragg, it was clear that I had to get my mind off Emma. There was no time to celebrate my birthday as six weeks of the preparation course was to start. Fail Special Forces Preparation Course and my dream of a career in the Army Special Forces would end.

This course focuses heavily on physical fitness. I was fit and strong, so this part was of no real concern. The other focus was land navigation. Each candidate was expected to demonstrate a reasonable proficiency. My prior experience was mostly navigating New York City, sometimes a challenge, but far removed from the expectations of this portion of the course. I was worried, but the instruction was good and clear. I passed this hurdle well within required proficiency.

My SFPC was now complete with a passing grade. I would move on to Special Forces Assessment and Selection (SFAS). This was a test of survival skills, with a strong emphasis on both physical and mental training. SFAS is considered to be the first real phase of Special Forces training. I certainly knew that I did well in the physical part. I was not as confident in the mental aspect. Anna was the smart one in our family. I should not have been worried as I was told my overall grade was among the best in our class. Maybe Anna just studied more.

While the course was ongoing, our mail was held until course completion. I had two letters. One was from Anna giving me news from home and her college studies. The other was post-marked Vilsek, Germany with Emma's return address. I never opened the letter. I kept it for some years, until Bethany became my life.

With the first training phase complete, I now moved to the Special Forces Qualification Course (SFQC). This qualification consisted of six phases lasting a little more than one year.

The first week was the Special Forces Orientation Course which was to give us a general understanding of missions and doctrine, Mission Command, unconventional warfare, and some of the history of Special Forces. Good information, but nothing to be tested about.

The next training would be for thirteen weeks to cover Special Forces common tasks, advanced special operations techniques, with survival, evasion, resistance and escape exercise. We all could realize how important this training was. Concentration was high.

The next phase, Collective Training, was the litmus test for soldiers hoping to make it through all training to graduation. Here, we were organized into squads to be inserted into a fictional country made up over a very large area. The country is in political turmoil, and we were required to navigate the region to complete a specific mission. The squads might come under fire.

My squad completed its mission with no casualties. This is when I knew, in a real wartime, I wanted to be with these guys. One that I could tell would always have my back was from a small town in Alabama. I remembered from basic training that an old sergeant talked of wanting boys from Alabama in a fire fight. He said they would never run and would fight to the end. He went on to laugh about the only problem being in peace time. They would sometimes get homesick and go absent without leave.

Next, the Regimental First Formation moved us from field work into classrooms. There were many small but important matters to learn. An emphasis was placed on how close we were to graduation.

The last training, twenty-five weeks of Language and Culture, was for us to demonstrate proficiency in a foreign language which we would select from a dozen or so offered. I had not taken a foreign language in high school. I found Italian was not offered for selection. I would most likely have been in a panic mode except that we were told, off the record by a young officer, that this requirement would not cause a failure. Even in the same country, there would be too many dialects to master, along with accents, and the Special Forces now relied on hiring locals for communications.

Spanish and French were thought to be the easiest to learn, but I selected German, as my time in Vilsek gave me a good background for this language. I would study hard while often thinking of the good days in Germany with Emma. I believe my entire class passed to the last week.

The final phase, Graduation, is one week of out-processing. At the end I could join my comrades in wearing the Green Beret as Special Forces soldiers.

There was one night of very serious drinking for our group before we separated to move on to the next duty assignment.

CHAPTER EIGHT

I was not surprised that my home base assignment for the Special Forces was Fort Bragg. The North Carolina base is the largest in the world and calls itself home of the Special Forces.

Fort Bragg had about fifty thousand army personnel living on post, with another twenty thousand or so off post in the city of Fayetteville. Being unmarried, I was assigned to a barracks housing enlisted men.

Training in the Special Forces never ends except when a group leaves on assignments of duty around the world. When this is to occur, there may be weeks or months of preparation if time allows. If there was not time, we performed the mission based on our months of readiness training for all contingencies.

During my time at Fort Bragg, the world was about as stable as it gets. There were a couple of assignments out of this country, but my group remained at this base for most of my years.

The surrounding area had nice parks, hiking trails, fishing and other outdoor activity, along with the waters and beaches of Cape Fear not too many miles away. None of this was particularly my "cup of tea". Maybe this would have been more appealing if I had acquired a wife and family.

Likewise, Fayetteville had little to offer an unmarried soldier. The best restaurant may have been a Red Lobster; the bars were much more expensive than the enlisted men's club on base; and there were few unmarried women (excepting the numerous prostitutes found outside the base gates). The movie theaters within the Fort were as good as those in the city. All of this left me searching for a life other than training.

I was lucky that I did have interests that made my army free time enjoyable. To start, physical fitness was most important to me personally as well as a general requirement of the Special Forces. I spent hours running inside and outside the base. While our daily training included exercise, I added more outside our work hours. At one point, I held the Fort Bragg record for the most "chin-ups" without stopping to rest.

Next came my love of boxing. There were great facilities to train and engage others in your weight class. Our officers were mostly men who enjoyed sports. My company commander had some college experience in the sport of boxing and asked me to represent the base in military boxing bouts. I fought a lot with much success, mostly winning with knock-outs.

The boxing expanded, with bouts against the best of other bases. My success continued, culminating with a challenge for the army championship against an undefeated officer stationed at Fort Riley, Kansas, with the 1st Infantry Division, "the Big Red One". The fight would take place at Fort Riley.

I realized the importance placed on this match when I was relieved of all duty assignments to train and prepare. When the time arrived, I flew to Kansas in a military aircraft with my company commander, two company sergeants who would serve as my "seconds" in the boxing ring, the Fort Bragg commanding general, and his next in command. I had never before spoken to a general, let alone a commanding general.

The military rivalry was apparent. This was the

Special Forces command versus the most elite Infantry division.

My opponent was a trim, black man, about my age, who appeared to be built of nothing but muscle. He had obtained his officer commission as a graduate of the United States Military Academy at West Point. I was told he had boxed in both high school and at the Academy.

I will not bore you with a round by round account. The match was twelve rounds, if it lasted that long. Over the course of the match, I was knocked to the ring floor twice, my opponent went down twice also, and we both were substantially cut, battered and bruised. At the conclusion of twelve rounds we hugged like brothers, showing the respect we each had for the other.

The judges ruled the bout a draw. One voted that I won by one point, one did the same in favor of my opponent, and the third found the points to be even. There was some talk of a rematch that never materialized. I felt comfortable that we were both happy not to fight each other again.

After physical fitness and boxing, my next

interest was playing poker. You may recall that I enjoyed playing for pennies with my parents and their friends. Games of poker are very common in all branches of the military. For enlisted men, who were paid once each month, in cash, payday always resulted in many games. If you were a very good player, your monthly income could be regularly increased.

In high school I had intently watched my parents play, noting the various techniques of folding hands not suitable for play, making bets with good hands, calling or raising bets by other players, and bluffing (betting in an effort to make your losing hand appear to be a winner in order to get the better hand to fold).

While in Germany, I had read several books on poker and observed the payday big games. Many players just like to gamble, not being willing to observe and study in order to play a winning game. I concluded I could play a winning game at the level of poker played in the military. My conclusion was correct. I spent many paydays, and other times when a game was available, winning a nice amount of extra money.

There was no supervision of the military games,

so one had to be very careful to be certain no player was cheating. On one occasion a soldier I did not know from another barracks joined the game I was in. There was no designated dealer. The deal of the hands was passed around to each player.

The new player would shuffle the deck of cards thoroughly before dealing. Too thoroughly I thought. On the hands he dealt, I noticed he always dealt himself winning aces. To confirm he was an accomplished cheat, I watched his expression when I folded queens I had been dealt before any one had bet. His expression told me he knew I had been dealt queens that would lose to his aces.

I called him outside to emphasize he would leave and not play in our barracks game again. He acted as if he wanted to fight. This would have suited me, but he backed off and left. I talked to the sergeant in charge of his barracks. I was pleased to be informed that this asshole was banned from playing in any game on our post.

I gradually gained a reputation as one of the best poker players at Fort Bragg. This did not go unnoticed to one Major who was also an excellent player. He played in regular games at the officer's club. As an enlisted man, I could not play there.

When off duty on some weekends, the Major would frequent the nearest casino that had poker tables. He invited me to go with him. The problem was that the games at the casino involved higher money stakes than I could afford. We reached an agreement that he would furnish money for me to play. I was to play very carefully and conservatively. If I won, he would have seventy-five percent of the winnings, but would cover all of any loss. A very good arrangement for me. However, I won consistently, and we both had a nice profit.

One of the problems when I was at Fort Bragg was the shortage of women to date, especially for enlisted men. At this point in time, it was not as usual for women to join the army as they would in later years. Many of those that did were married or married shortly after enlisting. There were a lot of civilian employees that were female, but most were married and, if not, were looking for companionship with officers.

A soldier could not leave the base without encountering a host of whores waiting just outside the gates. Whores were not my style although I will confess to a few liaisons when I really felt a need. Over time, I did manage some nice relations with civilian employees and once had a seven-or-eight month relationship with an attractive girl who had joined the military at age eighteen. This might have been long-term except that she was transferred to a duty station in Japan.

Leave away from the army was always nice. I would go to the Bronx to visit my family. The military was my career, but my parents, sister, and even the Bronx, were my home.

CHAPTER NINE

One trip home was particularly enjoyable. Anna was in her final year at Fordham and had an "off" weekend, meaning a weekend without a date. This was unusual for my very popular sister, but gave both of us an opportunity to catch up on where the other was in life.

We went to Tinker's Bar, a local "watering hole" popular with the college students to have a couple of beers and conversation. The couple of beers turned into quite a few, as we talked for hours.

Anna would graduate with a degree in Social Services. She was excited she could make a good living while helping the same people we had lived around that were so in need in the South Bronx.

I knew little about Fordham University, or about any university for that matter, so I asked for details. She told me Fordham was an old established Catholic and Jesuit school dating back to 1841. The total enrollment would be less than fifteen thousands students. She seemed to know a lot about the athletic programs which surprised me. That is, until she disclosed that she had two primary boyfriends, one a football player and the other on the basketball team.

The basketball player, who was from Brooklyn, had learned his skills as a white boy playing high school ball in the very strong New York City systems dominated by good, some great, black athletes. Fordham had football, basketball, baseball and soccer as scholarship sports. Anna's friend was not good enough for major caliber basketball, but played with enough skill to make the Fordham team.

Anna had surprised me with sports information, somewhat explained by the boyfriends, but much more in detail than I would expect even from a very smart young lady.

I was told that the Fordham Rams played basketball in Rose Hill Gymnasium, a facility seating thirty-two hundred, and being nationally the oldest campus arena still in use. The Rams were participants in the first college basketball game shown on television, a Madison Square Garden game, lost to the Pittsburg Panthers.

Turning to the other boyfriend, football player John Elliott, Anna's smile gave away her choice of a favorite. John was from Michigan where he was the best player on his small high school team. Being from a family of modest financial means, similar to ours, he needed a sports scholarship to attend college. While he was his team's best player, he was not of sufficient ability to be highly sought in the hotbed of Michigan football. John was a good student who considered Fordham the best college scholastically offering an opening on the football team.

The football home games were played in Jack Coffey Field, a stadium with a seating capacity of seven thousand. Compare this with a major college football program, such as Alabama, hosting games in Tuscaloosa before more than one hundred thousand fans.

The next night, Anna got me a date with one of her high school friends, and we returned to Tinker's for the evening. Her John was a pleasant young man, nice looking, and most polite. He was conversant, but did not dominate conversations, a good listener with genuine interest. I could see Anna's attraction. Even though she was dating freely, including the basketball player, I knew John could be long-term.

Anna would receive her degree with Highest Honors. Even with the most scholarship and financial aid made available to her, the high cost of a Fordham education left her owing a debt of over five thousand dollars. She broke into tears when I gave her the money to clear her debt. Being frugal in the military had not been difficult for me. Now my sister could begin life after college without the pressure of debt.

I was not able to attend Anna's graduation. I was sent with my Special Forces group on a mission to South America. I will not describe the purpose of our mission, which was a success, as this assignment remains classified as a secret military operation to the present. Though many years have passed since my military days, my respect and honor for the Special Forces and our Army compels my silence.

Later, as my story continues, you will know details about government actions, outside the military, in which I played an important part.

Anna sent me pictures of her graduation, and the

small gathering of friends at our home afterward. It was clear that the wine had flowed in a festive atmosphere. I will never forget the smile on our father's face.

CHAPTER TEN

With college degree in hand, Anna applied for employment with the Bronx section of the New York Department of Social Services. The entire New York State had fifty-eight Social Services Districts, the five Burroughs of the City of New York comprising one, and the other fifty-seven being one district for each of the counties.

I knew Anna sincerely wanted to help the people where she was raised. I also was certain that she was pleased to be working near Fordham as her football player was staying there to attend law school for a period of three more years.

With her school record, getting the job was just the formality of applying. She was granted her specific request to be assigned to Protective Services for Older Adults. This was a field which she emphasized in her college studies. Primarily, she would be dealing with neglect by family, caregivers or simply an older person alone who could not manage.

Anna had written an extensive college treatise on social service protection of the elderly. This writing was so good that her Professor sent copies to all of the New York offices for the Department of Social Services. She had demonstrated by interviews with a number of elderly that neglect could be beyond the normal failure to provide or allow access to food, shelter, clothing, heating, stimulation and activity, personal or medical care.

My caring sister had found additional areas of neglect. Her interviews of many elderly disclosed care given in a way the person did not like, not giving medication in the way prescribed, refusal of access to visitors, not accounting for cultural, religious, or ethnic needs, and ignoring or isolating the person. She wrote in definitive, convincing style.

Some caregivers, professional or family, did not know, while others failed to consider or care. And then there were some among the elderly who were alone trying to meet their own needs without assistance. Thus neglect could be intentional or unintentional, willful or just careless.

Her treatise spoke to evidence of neglect which

she had found. The elderly person could be dirty or unhygienic, sores or ulcers could be present, unexplained weight loss and accumulation of medicine not taken were signs, as were a reluctance to converse or interact.

If an elderly person was alone, without a caregiver, Anna found indicators of self neglect. Some were poor personal hygiene, dirty clothing or appearance, malnutrition and/or dehydration, hoarding, and keeping a large number of animals, typically cats or, less often, dogs.

Our mother had sent me a copy of Anna's treatise. I was, of course, impressed, but this was so "Anna", my caring, loving sister, not just to family, but to anyone she came in contact with.

After working for several months, she told me of some co-workers (always a few) who disliked her because of her writing, saying she was "a young, know-it-all, trying to prove how smart she was".

As most people, Anna did not like criticism without good cause, but she said if her writing helped one elderly person, she could take the flack. I told her that those being critical were likely poor employees who secretly felt what she had written applied or was directed to them.

CHAPTER ELEVEN

John, Anna's football player friend, had started his first year of law school, while she was working overtime in her Social Services employment. Both were very busy, but not too busy for each other. Their relationship was in an upward spiral. Her basketball player was no longer in contention, as John and Anna had become a steady couple. Anna was living at home with our parents while John was in on-campus housing.

People outside the New York area rarely know of the high academic standards at Fordham. These are maintained in its law school program. John was smart, but not brilliant like Anna, which was demonstrated by his first semester grades. He was ranked in the upper middle of his freshman class, certainly reasonable, but not sufficient to draw attention from any of the one hundred or so large, established New York firms. He would graduate with about the same class ranking.

Starting with the second law school semester, John and Anna decided they could afford a one-bedroom apartment near the campus. Though their parents would not have agreed, the younger generation had decided that marriage was not a prerequisite to living together. I was not surprised when a letter from Anna about twelve months later was to inform me that marriage was in the works.

When I went home my sister took over an hour telling me there were problems to be solved. Anna had attended the Catholic Church to the exclusion of others. John really had no religious preference, but had been raised in the Baptist Church of his hometown. His mother was dedicated to that church, a most important part of her life.

When Anna had visited Wolftown, Michigan with John, she found a nice small town of about twelve thousand, that seemed to have churches everywhere. The largest was First Baptist which was attended by John's mother and father.

By tradition, most weddings were held where the bride's parents lived. This did not necessarily mean that the wedding had to be at the church usually attended by the bride and her family. John's mother had taken Anna to her church to meet the Pastor. She did nothing to conceal her thoughts of the virtues of the Baptist religion. It was clear to see she would like the wedding to be in a Baptist Church. She had stopped just short of saying her grandchildren would be best served in the environment of the Baptist family.

John knew his mother was strong-willed. Anna told her intended of suspicion that, although Baptist was certainly his mother's first choice, she could have some anti-Catholic thoughts. Anna was going to do some research into Baptist and Catholic differences before they completed wedding plans that might create family problems at the outset of married life together. John told Anna how much he loved her, that how the wedding went forward was her choice, and he would back any decision.

Anna soon learned that one could spend years trying to understand all of the doctrine differences of these two churches. In fact, she concluded there were religious experts with years of study who could not agree on the doctrines of their one church, with no chance on agreeing to all of the differences between Baptist and Catholic. She decided to go simplistic and basic.

Following her careful study, Anna told John she

could not be sure, but would give him her best judgment.

It was clear and undisputed that both religions believed in and worshiped Jesus. Likewise, they both defended the sanctity of human life and the institution of marriage to be between one man and one woman (she joked that she was so pleased that John had been born with a penis).

The major differences she could glean from the mass of literature was the route to heaven, baptism and the seriousness of various sins. The Baptist belief was that one would receive God's grace solely through faith in Jesus Christ, by this faith alone. The Catholic belief differed in that to receive the grace of God and eternal salvation, one must receive the sacraments from the church. The Baptist position was that the sacraments are contrary to the teachings of the Bible, that grace is received directly from God because of belief in Jesus Christ, and not by going through the Catholic sacrament requirement. Thus a difference that appeared to Anna to be one that most likely cannot be reconciled.

Anna had found that there are seven sacraments in the Catholic religion. The first, and seemingly the most important, is baptism. Again a major difference. Catholics believe baptism is essential to grace and babies receive baptism. Baptists take a view that a child should not receive baptism until an age of some understanding, perhaps age seven or older.

Contrary to the Baptists, Catholics distinguish between the seriousness of various sins. Murder, adultery, stealing and lying are called mortal sins which must be confessed to a priest in order to receive forgiveness. Other less serious sins, known as venial sins, can be atoned for after death in a place called purgatory.

At this point, I told Anna my head was swimming with information I would never understand. The important thing was that she and John loved each other, and the old phrase "love conquers all" was applicable to their finding a solution.

I left to return to army life secure in my thought that my very smart sister would find a path through the maze.

About two weeks later I received another letter from Anna containing the resolution. She and John would marry in a civil ceremony including only me as their required witness. Neither set of parents would be notified until after the marriage. The excuse would be avoiding the cost of a formal church wedding. While there would be some immediate family disappointment, the logic of cost savings would be recognized. Our parents had no extra funds, and John's parents had been struggling to help him with law school expenses.

The Baptist Church would recognize a civil marriage. The Catholic would not, but there was a solution Anna had discussed with our priest at Our Lady of Mount Carmel Church. After a civil ceremony, the couple could seek to have their union officially recognized by the Catholic Church, a proceeding known as a "convalidation" of a marriage. She had been privately assured this would be no problem.

The married couple would attend both churches as time passed, not ruling out joining a third, with no rush to decision.

Anna, of course, had also researched having a civil union in New York. They would go to New York City Hall in Manhattan to obtain a license.

After a legally required wait of at least twenty-four hours, the three of us would go to the Marriage Bureau.

On the day they had selected, my sister put on her favorite Sunday "go to meeting" dress, John was in a dark suit and red tie, while I was in full army dress.

In the office of the clerk, identification was required from all of us, along with the marriage license. A ticket was then issued with a number. After some wait, the number was called for the final paperwork to be filled out. I signed, they signed, and the fee was paid. Now, just like the army, more waiting.

Eventually we were called to station five, presented the license to the clerk, and were to wait in the vestibule. There were two chapels or rooms. Finally there was a call by names into the room for the ceremony. The officiant performed the ceremony in less than two minutes. Anna and John exchanged rings and were now Mr. and Mrs. John Elliott. My sister had wanted to be known as Anna Elliott. In the hallway and in front of the building, I took a few pictures, and we boarded the subway back to the Bronx.

I left on my return trip to Fort Bragg, leaving the newly wed couple to work out informing both sets of parents of their new status in life.

Anna later told me that the parents were reasonable and loving. The cost of a formal wedding was not mentioned, but Anna felt the civil ceremony relieved some pressure that would have been felt if they had proposed a church, invitations, and wedding guests.

John's parents, his mother in particular, were aware their church recognized the civil ceremony. They avoided saying this was much more acceptable than would have been a Catholic ceremony.

Our parents were worried about the lack of a church ceremony until Anna explained the "convalidation" that would take place.

CHAPTER TWELVE

When John entered his senior year of law school, the students at the top of his class were receiving offers of employment from the large New York City firms. Those close to the top were in the interview process by the same firms. If they were not hired, they would be highly considered by the next level of New York firms. John was in the upper middle of his class academic rank. He had no New York connections to be considered on that basis. If he wanted to stay to work in New York, he would be dependent on the employment services at Fordham.

There was a town in northern Ohio about thirty-five miles south of Wolftown, Michigan. Monville, Ohio had a population of some forty-thousand with a diversified business community. Robert Collins was a middle-aged widower, a sole-practice lawyer, majority owner and Chairman of the Board of Directors of the largest local bank. His only child, son Tim, had been installed as an Assistant Vice-President, who would, with sufficient experience, become the bank President.

John and Tim had a friendship dating back to high school football as Monville and Wolftown played on an annual basis. Although rivals, they became close friends, and on occasion traveled back and forth to spend week-ends together.

Robert Collins had a large, thriving legal practice, almost too much for one lawyer. A wealthy man, he did not need or want to continue working for more than two or three years. Tim had stayed in touch with John and suggested that his father might want to interview him.

At Mr. Collins request, John agreed to come to Monville for a meeting. This was just to be the two for the business discussion, with Tim to join for a social dinner. Anna would wait to come the next time if there was mutual interest.

John met with Mr. Collins for over three hours before a pleasant dinner at the Monville Country Club. It was just the three men as Tim's wife would wait for Anna to come if an agreement might be reached. Mr. Collins listened while Tim and John recalled their teen years in athletic competition, dating, and spending weekends together. It was obvious that Tim would enjoy having John in

Monville.

John stayed the night in Monville, to return to the Bronx the next morning. The arrangement was that Mr. Collins would consider all they had discussed, give each time to think, and allow John and Anna time to talk over all that such a move would involve.

In his rental car, the drive was over eight hours, and a bus or train would have taken longer. The distance would be a concern for Anna. Only after their marriage had she given any real consideration to circumstances that might result in a move from New York. The proximity to her parents was most important in Anna's life. Also, she really enjoyed her job.

I had a short discussion with Anna about this possibility when she told me of the wedding plans. I knew my sweet sister well. She loved our parents dearly. Added to this were the problems that went with their health and advancing ages. But if she loved a man enough for marriage, as with John, he would be the primary focus of her life.

Anna could tell almost immediately how excited her husband was over the possibility of good employment after graduation. They talked a lot about the different ramifications. She was pleased at the amount of time John spent in consideration of her feelings. They would continue to talk, but would wait on the contact from Mr. Collins before deciding if Monville might be in their future.

It was a long week until John received a letter that detailed an offer from Mr. Collins. The beginning salary was higher than expected. There was a Country Club membership with dues paid and a promise from Mr. Collins that Anna would have a Social Services employment consistent with hers in the Bronx. If the offer was acceptable, they should both come to Monville to be certain Anna could feel at home and be happy.

The trip to Monville was merely a formality. Anna knew her husband wanted this opportunity. She would never consider they should deviate from something very important to John.

When they arrived, Tim's wife, Bridget, took over with Anna. They discussed life in Monville, toured the town, and dined at the Country Club with six women friends Bridget had invited. It was a warm beginning to small town life.

CHAPTER THIRTEEN

My intention was an army career of at least twenty years, more likely twenty-five or thirty. After about a dozen years, one telephone call from my mother was life changing. My father had been diagnosed with terminal lung cancer. He was no longer able to work with a life expectancy of only a few months. Mother was so distraught that she could hardly talk.

I told her I would be there, taking emergency leave, and boarded the next train to New York. I arrived in the Bronx about the same time as Anna.

The family situation was desperate. Our father could no longer work. Mother was not leaving him alone, so she had closed the grocery store. I soon learned the grocery was struggling financially. Movement of the large chain stores into the area, with prices my parents could not meet, had siphoned off many previously loyal customers. Local convenience could not handle the challenge of lower pricing.

My parents had recently taken out a mortgage loan secured by the store building. The building, their only financial asset, was now at a serious risk of loss.

My thoughts were all over the place. Mother had worked in the grocery along side our father from the inception, but she dealt with customers and had little knowledge of the business side, payroll, taxes, licenses, inventory, cash flow, and so on. If the grocery was lost, how would mother live financially after her husband was gone. She certainly could not move as their apartment was affordable only because of the New York rent control laws.

Anna was understandably upset as we talked at length with no solution. She was living hours away, working five days per week, and had just learned she was pregnant. Certainly she would visit as often as possible, but visits could not solve our mother's business and financial problems. There was no other solution, I had to step up to the plate.

I returned to Fort Bragg, met with my Commanding Officer, filled out the necessary paperwork, and received a family hardship discharge from the military. I will have to confess I cried

when I received the discharge papers. The proudest
moment in my life, becoming a Special Forces
member of the United States Army, was now history.

Back in the Bronx, I reopened the grocery store
in an effort to salvage the business. Thinking back, I
am sure part of the problem was my lack of business
training but, whatever, after months of trying, I
could not bring the business to a profitable level.
The bank loan was well in arrears with foreclosure
on the horizon.

In the Army, I had developed a friendship with a
"good old boy" from the south part of Georgia. I
recalled a conversation over a couple of beers when
he spoke of the plight of his grandparents during the
great depression of the 1930's. They were in a
similar situation as my parents with a failing
business, large mortgage on their building, and no
means or hope of paying the mortgage debt. This
was solved when his grandfather, in the desperate
situation, set fire to the building. The insurance
proceeds paid the debt and provided enough surplus
money to get the family through the hard times.
Fortuitous fires that paid mortgage and bank debt
were quite common in the South during the
depression. As most of the insurance companies at

that time were headquartered in the North, a common reference to the fires that burned insured buildings was "selling out to the Yankees".

It was only several days, after my recollection of the conversation with my Georgia friend, that a fire consumed the building and contents of the grocery. Though arson was suspected, I had been very careful, and no proof was found. The insurance proceeds canceled my parents debt, with a little extra money. Our father died two weeks later knowing mother was out of debt.

I was now a criminal, an arsonist. Thinking back to the time I killed the would-be robber after he was no longer a threat, I was most likely also a murderer. The once proud Special Forces Green Beret had fallen to a level I would have not thought possible.

It was too late to change the past. I could try to mentally justify where I was in life, but necessity required that I work out some plan for my future. I needed a source of income for my personal support and to help my mother who now had only social security income.

Mother was so sad after our father's death I

thought she would have liked to have passed away with him. There was a saving grace as she could look ahead to becoming a grandmother when Anna produced her expected healthy baby.

CHAPTER FOURTEEN

The Fifteenth United States Congressional District, located entirely in the Bronx, is ranked as the poorest in the entire country. By contrast, the Twelfth District is our country's richest, located primarily in the Manhattan Upper East Side, with parts of Queens and Brooklyn.

Why is the Fifteenth so poor? It is almost entirely occupied by "people of color", primarily Hispanics and Latinos, many first or second generation immigrants, without good english language, formal education, or employment skills. Public housing is the home of the majority and unemployment is rampant.

Most of the people have no credit standing or history. Bank loans are not available without good credit reports. A bank term for these poor people is that they are "credit invisible".

New York law is among the strongest in the United States with its prohibitions against predatory lending. Every lender is required to have a license.

Interest charges are limited. Several types of short-term loans are prohibited. An example is the prohibited "pay-day" loan by which a loan for a few days, maybe a week or two, is due to be repaid at the time the borrower is paid through employment. Another is the "bad check" loan where the borrower gives the lender a check drawn on insufficient funds or even with no account. If the loan is not repaid, the lender files or threatens criminal charges for issuing a worthless check.

Without access to legal credit in the ghetto, the poor usually try to borrow from family or friends. If this source in not available or exhausted, their only source is the neighbor money lenders. These lenders are not licensed, charge illegal interest rates, and are present to prey on the desperate borrowers.

In the Spanish-speaking areas, these are referred to as "prestamistas", Spanish for money lenders, and sometimes as "shadow banks of the barrio". The word "shadow" is most appropriate as these lenders do not operate from traditional offices. They are found by local knowledge and word of mouth. When law enforcement is present, they simply disappear and wait for other opportunity.

Being from the Bronx, I was generally familiar with this type of lender, commonly called "loan shark". As a teenager, my father had admonished me to never take a loan from a shark. He told me of a nice older woman from a barrio, Anita Ramos, who dreamed of having a florist business. She had no credit, but found a prestamista who made her a five thousand dollar loan, payable at one hundred dollars each week. She had no understanding of interest charges, but managed to pay the weekly payments, only to find that at the end of one year she still owed the entire principal loan sum of five thousand dollars. When the lender threatened to harm her grandson, she continued making weekly payments for several year until she died.

Anita's lender was a small-time punk working for Anthony "Fat Tony" Sarleno, a mafia underboss notorious as a loan shark.

You may now be wondering why my story has wandered into the plight of the poor without sources of legal loans. Well, remember that I was in dire circumstances after burning my parents building. I had to find a job, a source of income.

Enter Ricardo Lopez, a man I had known only

casually in high school. He asked to have a confidential conversation with me. He was a small man, thin, with dark hair, who came quickly to the point. He had received a large money settlement from an automobile accident. All of his life had been lived in Bronx public housing. He knew the people and the constant need for small loans without credit.

Ricardo wanted to be an illegal money lender in the area of the Bronx he knew well. Pointing out that he was not physically imposing, he would not be able to frighten borrowers into paying. He wanted me as a business partner because of my reputation as a tough boxer with army special training. I would call on borrowers when payments were past due to emphasize that payment should be made.

When I responded that I did not want to hurt people, Ricardo was very persuasive. He explained how he would be careful to make loans just to people he knew something about, those he would expect to find some way to pay. Only when he could not persuade would I come into the picture.

We talked a long time. Ricardo explained how

much money could be made even after factoring in losses. Someone borrows ten dollars for a week, they pay back twelve. Borrow one hundred for a month, pay back one hundred twenty. On and on, the figures were staggering.

His offer impressed me as extremely fair. Only his money would be at risk. I would have the risk of physical altercations. If we were arrested, he would pay all legal fees. Then, the real kicker. I would receive one-third of all the profits. If his figures was close to correct, I would be making more money than any employment I could find in the city.

The deal was made. If I could avoid arrest, I would provide for Mother and live better than I imagined possible. Now I could add to my resume of shame: "Loan Shark."

CHAPTER FIFTEEN

My adventure into the illegal loan business went generally well. I did not get arrested, killed or badly hurt. I made more money than I had imagined, a lot more.

Ricardo was very good at this business. His thought processes in making determinations as to good loan customers were strong. He often said that we needed to find borrowers who would want to pay, but who also had enough financial discipline to find a means to pay. Slow pay was alright, the interest kept accumulating. Ricardo would talk frequently to these people, encouraging payment and also offering advice on saving to pay.

When payments stopped, it was my time to go to work. I knew the borrower as Ricardo would introduce me as his assistant when the loan was made. I would usually start by talking about how fair Ricardo had been when money was an immediate problem, and they should remember there could always be a time when another loan might be needed. This approached often failed. So, I would move on to the stronger methods.

I explained I did not want to physically hurt them, but I was paid to collect and would do so however I had to. If their reaction was negative, I would take an arm, press hard, and push them to a wall. If one fought back, a strong punch to their midsection was effective. I would leave at that point with an admonishment to have the money when I returned.

Returning was my real danger. The borrower in default might have a weapon. He might have solicited one or more friends to attack me. I had to take care to be ready for anything. My reputation for being tough was important.

A simple defense for the borrower would be to call the police to report my participation in an illegal loan activity. However, in the ghetto areas of our operations, the police were considered an enemy by most of the poor population.

If "roughing up" the borrower did not work, I would move on to the method I really disliked. I would threatened to harm a family member. Sometimes I had to confront a brother, uncle or father. Sometimes I made the threat toward a female in the family, but I can say, in some little defense of the way I made money, that I never harmed a sister, aunt or mother.

I was able to physically prevail in a one-on-one altercation. A few times I was attacked by two or three men. While I managed to handle these situations, I was sometimes injured, once or twice experiencing a trip to a hospital emergency room.

I had a good amount of free time between involvements in our loan business. Ricardo collected a lot more often than many in this shadow business. He paid me on a regular basis. Thus, I had money. No taxes, no deductions, just cash money.

I had time and the money to participate in my favorite activity for entertainment. This was the game of poker I had first learned in the penny home games with my parents and had later polished skills and learning in the military service.

Poker is a type of game with many different variations. The constant is the rules of the card combinations that determine which wins over another. In the majority of games, the winner is the highest/best hand of five cards. To a lesser extent, there are some games in which the winner is the lowest/worst hand. Then there are high/low games in which the best and worst share the "pot" (the amounts that have been bet by the players) equally.

The games of my parents, and when I began playing in the Army, were "draw and stud" played in several variations. But, by the time I had money from the shark business, there was a game that had taken over the poker playing world. The name of this game was "Texas Holdem".

As the name would imply, the game originated in the State of Texas. Gambling was illegal, but this type of poker was a common activity throughout the state. There were numerous professional players who traveled, usually by automobile, stopping wherever a substantial money game could be found.

Games might be played in private homes, their outbuildings or garages. Motel games were not uncommon. The games were not always honest. An arriving player had to be aware that cheating could occur. If the out-of-town player was winning, he might be threatened if trying to leave with a large amount of money, There was no regulation. Gambling without regulation often produces these types of dangerous situations. The traveling players had to be constantly aware.

One of the best known and best players was Doyle Brunson. For many years, he traveled the State of Texas as a professional gambler. When this game eventually moved to the Las Vegas casinos, and from there throughout the legal casinos and poker rooms of the world, Brunson became a celebrity in this hugely popular game of Texas Holdem.

Brunson has written books on the proper play of this game, but has also delved into his history as a road gambler. In reading one of his books, I had become interested in the life of Texas gamblers in the seedy days before legal regulation.

Brunson spoke of the perils of trying to leave after winning large amounts in some games on the road. Losers, who could be angry, often drunk, would sometimes demand that he continue to play, with threats if he insisted on leaving with his winnings. To counter such situations, which were not uncommon, he traveled with his wife who would wait in their car. If he was winning enough that danger was likely, he would go to the door to signal her.

She would then come to the room armed with a shotgun to escort her husband, and the money, to their car.

Brunson was not the only Texas gambler to attain celebrity status after the game exploded in popular appeal. Aside from the cash games, poker tournaments emerged in the casinos, first attracting dozens of players, later evolving into hundreds and sometimes thousands. In the large tournaments millions could be awarded to the winners. Television coverage sparked interest, particularly among younger players who could learn the game playing on the internet.

I never cared for the tournaments where you could be eliminated early on, losing the entry fee. My preference was cash games where one could keep playing by adding more money after suffering an early loss.

By this point in time, New York City had dozens of poker rooms. A few were very nice though the majority were small, often located in bad areas where rent was lower, featuring only one table without amenities. I was not internet educated, so I selected the small rooms to play to learn the new rage which was often the only game available.

With knowledge of the basic rules governing which high hand would win in a comparison with others, you could learn to play Texas Holdem in an hour or less. Then you could spend a lifetime trying to learn to play well in competition with others. It was the seeming simplicity of the game that made it so attractive. Though I was a good overall poker player, I had a learning curve in this new game which took many months and several substantial losses to reach a winning level.

In Holdem each player at the table would be dealt two cards. A round of betting was allowed with an option to fold the hand, to call the amount bet, or to raise double or more of the original bet. This was the first skill level, knowing when the two cards were of sufficient value to justify continuing in the hand and how best to continue. Next three cards were dealt face up on the table (called the flop) with more betting allowed. For those still in the hand, a forth card (the turn) was dealt face up with more betting. If there was a bet which no one called, the hand was over with the pot awarded to the last bettor. Otherwise, a fifth card (the river) went on the table face up. Same betting procedure, and if a bet was called, the hands were exposed with the winning hand being the highest combination of the two cards in hand with the five common cards on the table. In other words, playing any five of the seven.

It sounds simple, doesn't it ?

CHAPTER SIXTEEN

I could never have imagined how my love of the game of poker would make such a change in my life. So, on with my story.

After I had learned enough to begin winning on a regular basis at the new game, I wanted to move from the dingy small rooms. The several larger rooms, with three tables in play, offered good food and a bar with free drinks served by very pretty young women. There were required reservations with a waiting list. I finally got a seat to play in a high end room on the lower end of the East Side.

Seated across from me at the table was a man with Italian features, about my age, perhaps a few years older. He appeared a few inches taller than me with a slender, athletic body.

The game was no-limit Texas Holdem. In no-limit, anyone at any time in the play could bet any amount or all of the money they had in front of them. There were ten players with a dealer at each table. A player could start with whatever amount of money they select (represented by poker chips purchased) and then add by purchasing additional chips as the game progressed. Nine of the players, including me, bought in for five hundred to one-thousand dollars in chips. The exception was the man I have described across the table from me. He bought in for five thousand.

There is a reason for wanting to have a much larger amount (your stack) than the other players at the table. A few just want to show off a large amount of cash, but the primary purpose is to intimidate the other players. By having a larger stack, the player can make bets at any time large enough to threaten another player that he could lose all of his chips in one hand.

The difficulty is the large stack player will probably bet often. When he does so, he could have the best hand at the table, or be "bluffing", that is betting like he has the best hand to induce the other players to fold, allowing him to take the pot without disclosing his actual two cards. This technique can be very effective, especially against inexperienced players or those short on money.

The large stack player at our table was very good

at diagnosing when other players had hands not strong enough to risk all of their stack. He soon was several thousand ahead.

I was not getting good starting cards, folding a lot, but watching the play carefully. Then I was dealt the ace of hearts and five of spades, not a great start, but enough to call a small bet which was made. The flop was a two of clubs with the three and queen of hearts. The large stack bet about the amount in the pot. He could have a queen, but I decided to see another card as my ace could pair or any four would give me a low straight (ace through five). The turn card was an eight, no help to me, but I decided to call another pot size bet. The river card was the seven of hearts, again no help to me, but would make a winning flush (five heart cards) if I had two hearts.

It was now decision time. I had about six hundred left in chips with about that much in the pot. The big stack did not bet as a heart flush would beat his hand. I decided he must have a pair of queens which I knew would win against my hand of only an ace high. However, I also knew he had been watching my previous conservative playing style. This was my moment. I said "all in" meaning in poker language that I was betting all my chips. He thought over this for over a minute, carefully going over the order of cards and bets. After this period of thought, he turned over one of his cards, the queen I suspected, before folding his hand to allow me to take the pot.

As he folded, he told me that he was certain I had stayed in the hand to try to draw a flush and was lucky to do so. In response to his arrogance, I disclosed both of my cards so he would know I had bet big with nothing to beat his queens, a total bluff that had worked.

His expression turned hard, his eyes focused on me in a steady stare. At one point I thought he might come across the table after me. Then, in a few more seconds, he said, "You know, I like you. You have guts. Come with me to the bar, let's have a drink and get acquainted." Such was the beginning of a friendship that has lasted to this day.

CHAPTER SEVENTEEN

At the poker room bar, my friend-to-be introduced himself as Giovanni Fanucci, to be called "Nucci". I returned the introduction. Nucci, upon hearing my name, surprised me by saying he knew that name to be the partner of Ricardo Lopez in the small loan business. I don't know if I looked shocked, but I certainly was. How could he know?

Nucci explained that he was involved with an organization that included a small loan business. Ricardo was smart enough to seek permission before opening his business in competition. A small operation outside the organization could be good in moving law enforcement focus in another direction, so Ricardo was approved. Without approval, he would have been in danger along with his partner.

Nucci never used the word "Mafia" in our conversation, but he knew that did not have to be stated for me to know.

Nucci was born and still lived in the "Little Italy" section of East Harlem on Manhattan Island, maybe fifteen to twenty minutes by subway from my "Little Italy" in the Bronx. As had mine, his grandparents had immigrated from Italy in search of a better life.

Nucci was married and lived with his wife not far from the home of his parents. He was head of a combined group of several local unions. Compared with the rest of the large cities in the United States, New York was heavily union organized, about double the union membership of any other other city. The unions were very active in opposition to any non-union company doing business with the city government.

I recalled from my childhood that the Manhattan Italian section was known for the notorious 116th Street Mob, a large criminal group that controlled the area in a wave of crime that lasted for years. If I had thought about the Mob, I suppose I would have associated it with the Mafia, but I really do not know. I did now wonder if Nucci's parents or grandparents were among these criminals. Curious certainly, but I would never ask.

We surrendered our seats at the poker table to sit, drink and continue talking at the bar.

The days of the cellular phone had arrived. We exchanged numbers with agreement to stay in contact. All in all, a very interesting evening.

CHAPTER EIGHTEEN

Within two weeks, I received a call from Nucci. We would meet at the same poker room at five o'clock the next Saturday night. We were to play until nine when he had a surprise for the remainder of the night. I was, of course curious, but could tell he really wanted me to wait. I did ask about getting a seat at a table in this popular and somewhat exclusive poker room. I had to wait some weeks to get in for my previous visit. Nucci explained my seat was reserved at his request. I gathered his request carried a lot of weight.

I was in my seat the next night when Nucci arrived. I was starting with a purchase of one thousand in chips while the floor manager brought Nucci five thousand. The others at the table, including me, had paid cash for their chips. I noticed that my friend only told the manager his amount without tendering any money. I believe he was the only player in the room allowed to play on credit.

I played my usual careful, conservative game. I

stayed out of large money hands in which Nucci was involved. He continued to make "over-bet" amounts on many pots. Everyone at the table knew he could not have a big hand on so many deals, but a lot of their money would be lost if they selected to call at the wrong time. I was going to avoid any major confrontation involving just the two of us.

With the time approaching, Nucci called the floor manager to cash our chips as we left our seats. It appeared he had won three to four thousand while I was happy to be eight hundred ahead.

At exactly nine o'clock, two very attractive young women walked through the poker room door, probably twenty-four or twenty-five years old. They were the surprise for the remainder of the night. Both would be deemed a "sports model" by most all men, but one especially appealed to me. I was more than pleased when the introductions indicated she would be my evening companion. Her name was Bethany. The other was Margo.

Nucci hailed a cab which took our foursome to the Majestic World Hotel, a very high-end small hotel in mid-town Manhattan. We were escorted to a top floor two bedroom suite with a full bar and small portions of cocktail food. Each of the girls took their overnight bag to a different bedroom. They returned to find Nucci had opened two bottles of very nice champagne.

The conversation was light and pleasant with flowing champagne. This was followed by a nice Oregon pinot noir with a small amount of food. At that point, Nucci excused himself to retire with Margo to a bedroom. I really wanted this time to talk with Bethany. She and Margo were a far distance from the street whores in the South Bronx or those waiting outside the gates of Fort Bragg.

Bethany and Margo roomed together in a dormitory at New York University. They were both beginning their final year of law school. Bethany was from a rural community in Iowa and an honor graduate of Iowa State University. She had several offers to attend law schools, but was intrigued by an offer from New York University. After consideration, she decided to see life in the Big Apple while continuing her education.

From the start money was a problem. She had a nice scholarship, but not enough for a full ride, and certainly not in one of the most expensive cities in the world. Her parents were working class, her father in a factory and mother in a restaurant. They helped financially as they could, but there were two younger children in a home with a mortgage.

By her senior year all college loan funds had been exhausted. She had to consider dropping out of school. Margo was in the same situation. They had spent a long day going to banks. All answers were the same. They already had too much debt, no assets, no income, and a law license was at least one year away.

Late in that afternoon, they had walked into a bar for beer to talk out their plight. The semi-dark room was empty except for two men dressed in suits and three college age boys. Their beer had just been placed on the table when the boys began harassing them. One was particularly drunk. He was such a nuisance they were considering leaving when one of the men walked over to tell the boys to back off or leave.

The drunk boy rose to push the man. In a flash he was on the floor bleeding profusely from a broken nose. When the other two came out of their seats, the second man in a suit was pointing a very

large pistol at them. The boys carried their friend
out to the street.

The first man (now known to the girls as Nucci)
could not apologize enough. He explained the bar
was not a college hangout. The boys had just
wandered in. Their beer and food for the remainder
of the evening would be complimentary. While the
bar did not appear as a fine restaurant, it produced
some the best Italian pizza in New York.

Broke, tired and hungry, Bethany and Margo
accepted the beer and pizza offer. By the time a
second beer was consumed, the pressure of the day
had Bethany in tears. Nucci came back to the table
to offer assistance. Wiping back tears, she told the
entire story of frustration.

The next morning a package was delivered with a
note. The package contained two identical, very
expensive, watches. The note was from Nucci.
The gift was stated to be from the bar. The
remainder of the note was an invitation. For the
following evening at seven o'clock he had a table for
three at a restaurant they knew to be the most
expensive Italian in the city. He disliked eating
alone and truly hoped they would join him, no

obligation except conversation.

She and Margo were not naive. After much discussion, they decided to go regardless of any motive for the invitation. The note stated a driver would be in the lobby of their dorm at fifteen minutes before seven in anticipation that they might accept.

On the drive to the restaurant, Margo asked the driver who he worked for. His short answer was "the company".

Nucci was seated when they arrived. The girls immediately noticed their department store dresses would not have been considered for wear by the older females at surrounding tables. Nucci was pleased they had worn the gift watches.

Champagne was at the table. As was customary in elite restaurants, the menu given to women had no prices. They were asked to order dinner before a wine was recommended by the waiter. Each had no clue as to wine parings, but two bottles of red wine arrived shortly before the food. Looking at the bottles, Nucci seemed satisfied with the waiter's choices.

After the meal, while waiting for dessert and after-dinner drinks, Nucci began the expected explanation of why they were invited. He told of being involved in a large business operation that, for security reasons, would remain unknown to them. Business men from other cities often visited New York with entertainment being expected. Two young and pretty girls would be excellent escorts for such visitors. If they would be agreeable to serve two nights each month, his business would pay their final year tuition, room, board, books and provide additional funds for normal expenses.

What would be expected? They would have cocktails and meals with the visitors, attend shows, theater, opera, and yes, they would be expected to spend the night and have sex.

Nucci then stopped, asking the girls not to respond until the next day. He added he would be one of the two the first night. He would give then give them a direct contact number if anything should happen that required his attention. They would have total protection from any overbearing visitor.

Bethany and Margo stayed awake most of the

night considering the offer. It boiled down to becoming very expensive whores in exchange for payment of the remainder of their law school expenses. While they should be shocked at such a proposal, there was something about Nucci's demeanor that left them feeling that he actually cared, or at least, his promise of protection was genuine.

They considered the norm for college dating. The boy would pay for drinks, also for a meal, and expect sex. Maybe not after the first or second date, but soon sexual favors were common. Bethany and Margo were not virgins by any means and often followed the college norm. They concluded that the primary difference between college dates and Nucci's visitors was the magnitude of the drinks, meals and entertainment, and the fact that sex was required, not an option.

Bethany had tears in her eyes as she concluded telling me of how she and Margo became escorts. She was concerned that she should not have told me. She was afraid Nucci would be angry.

I told Bethany that any conversation we had, or might later have, was just between the two of us. I was not one of the visitors, but a good friend in New York who Nucci had invited. I was very pleased she was now able to complete her dream of becoming a lawyer. I knew much about dreams that had faded because of circumstances in life.

I said it was now time for bed. I wanted her to understand that she was released from the sexual requirement. I was so happy when she replied that on this night she was looking forward to sex.

CHAPTER NINETEEN

When we awoke, Nucci was gone and Margo had made coffee in the living area. We ordered breakfast before a long conversation about the evening.

Margo was inquisitive about everything. She said "If I'm going to be a whore, I would like to know something about the man or men who are selecting who I am to fuck. Obviously, last night was different from what I expected, and I presume future "dates" will not be limited to you and Nucci". I responded that "Nucci and I are friends. We are not business partners. Being included in the evening was a surprise to me, but a most pleasant surprise. However, I have no control or input as to the future of your arrangement. I know from Bethany that the two of you are doing what is necessary in your circumstances, and I want both of you to know that I really understand. Badly needing money, I have entered a business that is both illegal and immoral. Never say whore again. You have made a necessary business decision that does not hurt other people, as my business does every day."

Breakfast arrived before the conversation could be extended. After eating, I called the front desk about charges and was told that all had been taken care of. When we parted, Bethany and I exchanged cellphone numbers with a clear understanding of no obligation.

Back in the Bronx, I called Nucci to thank him for the great evening. When he asked about Bethany, I responded that she was a genuinely nice person that I was really attracted to. Nucci laughed before telling me that when we became closer friends great evenings would be provided without obligation. In return for this particular evening, vigorish (interest charge) would be required. The "vig" was that I would help him win in a big poker game to be held in a few days.

This was a private game to be held in a residence in Brooklyn. The two of us with the house owner would be the only players from New York. The other seven were from various parts of the country with business interest in the Big Apple. The minimum starting amount for the game was one hundred thousand dollars. The maximum was two hundred thousand, but losers could replenish their stacks at any time. Nucci would provide all of the three hundred thousand. He would absorb any loss, but would take all of the winnings for both of us. I might get a small share if he did very well.

I was to play a mostly conservative game, avoiding big pots unless I held a very good hand. There would always be a few hands where I held cards that went with the common cards so well that I could not lose. On those hands, I would secretly signal Nucci to make a very large bet that could, with his reputation, well be a total bluff. Most often other players with good hands would call, or even raise, Nucci's bet. In the end, I would show a winning hand, taking the large pot, while Nucci would just fold his hand without showing what he actually held. We would have to be very careful to conceal our cheating as discovery in this game could get you killed.

I would be introduced as an associate of Nucci. The people in this game did not ask questions of each other. We would get our signals settled on the ride to Brooklyn. There would be an open self-service bar. We would always have drinks at the table, but just pretend to be consuming alcohol with only soda or tonic.

With the poker game conversation concluded, he told me that I had done well not to mention his wife when he was with Margo. In his organization there was a marital code. The wife was required to be totally faithful to the marriage. If she cheated with another man, the man would be killed. Divorce was not allowed. There were too many facts that could not be disclosed in court proceedings. The husband was allowed to have other women, but never in situations that would embarrass his wife. The wife would, of course, know what was going on. As a dutiful wife, she would always adhere to the time honored code of allowed infidelity. Since the early days of the mafia in Sicily, the man was dominant in the marriage.

CHAPTER TWENTY

The ride to the poker game was in a limo with a driver that would wait for me and Nucci until we were ready to leave. With our signals settled, the car arrived at a very large home in an expensive section of Brooklyn.

Introductions were short. Only first names were used. The host was the homeowner who collected the cash money, giving out chips in exchange to be used in the game. A professional dealer was provided. The bar was stocked with liquor of all kinds, numerous beers, and several bottles of wine. On a table was an assortment of food.

The poker table was high quality with chairs to match. With little conversation, the game was on.

For the first several hours, I got nothing in the way of good cards. Then I managed to win a few hands, increasing my stack to a little over three hundred thousand. Nucci was playing his usual game, a lot of betting coupled with his common way of bluffing on many hands. Several of the players were men with a lot of money and much less skill in the game. Nucci was dominating them to be winning a good amount.

Over six hours, into what was to be an eight hour game, there had not been a hand where our signals could be used. Then a miracle hand occurred. I was dealt two jacks. Nucci made his usual starting bet. The two best of the other players called his bet along with me. These two had the most chips of anyone at the table.

The flop of three was two jacks and a king. I had flopped four jacks, almost impossible to beat, so my signal went out. Nucci made a medium size bet, with both players calling. I did not raise at this point. The turn card was a heart which went with two other hearts from the flop. If a player had two hearts a flush would be made, a very good hand. Nucci made a bet of about the amount in the pot, the next player called, followed by an "all in" bet by the next. Of course I called with all the money I had. Nucci folded. The other player sighed, thought a long time, and called the bet. He had the heart ace and hoped for another heart to make the highest flush. The river card was not relevant. I had won a pot with more than six hundred thousand from the two players. With such a huge win, I just sat in my seat the remainder of the game without risking the money.

When the game ended, Nucci had also won, so in combination we had a profit of slightly over eight hundred thousand. We talked about the hands on the way back while downing several shots of "fireballs" from a bottle placed in the car for the ride.

Our driver took Nucci home first. I had not seen his very nice home before. It was quite late so an invitation to come in was not expected. He exited the car with more than one million in cash. There had been no talk of any share of the winnings for me.

Two weeks went by without any call from Nucci. I was beginning to question if we had the friendship I believed existed. Then a call came. I was told to be ready for a weekend trip to Connecticut. I was to bring no money, all expenses paid. I should have a suit for formal dining, casual wear for the days, and a bathing suit. When I started to ask questions, he interrupted to give me the time to expect the limousine, said good-bye, and concluded the call.

CHAPTER TWENTY-ONE

On Friday, when the limo arrived, I have never been more surprised. Seated in the back with Nucci were Bethany and Margo. We were on our way for two nights at the Mohegan Sun in Connecticut.

Nucci poured four glasses of a very nice white wine. He then told us to sit back, relax, and listen to what he had to say. No questions until he finished talking.

He told the girls that he had few friends. His business was very confidential, friends must trust each other, and over the years he had found few who could be totally trusted in all situations. I was so very pleased to learn his thoughts as to our relationship. I had lived my life without close friendships and had grown found of Nucci.

He continued by telling Bethany and Margo that I had recently helped him in a business matter that resulted in at least four times the profit he had expected. Their tuition, room, meals, and all other expenses that could be prepaid for their last year of college had been paid. They would find in their checking accounts liberal deposits for any other expenses including support until they could take the bar examination after graduation. While their financial arrangement was just with him, they should know that he was using some of my profit share to meet his obligation.

He went on to say that he could tell that I liked both of them, Bethany in particular, and would not have approved the escort arrangement if I had been given a vote. Because of his friendship with me, the money was being changed to a loan with the escort obligation canceled. Additionally, the so-called loan would be like many student loans of that time for which there is little expectation of payment. Actually, in this case, repayment would not be accepted.

He concluded by saying we were on a two hour trip to Uncasville, Connecticut. There we would find the Mohegan Sun hotel and casino. The facility was a thirty-four story building with three casinos, several show rooms, and more than forty bars, restaurants, and cafes. Upon arrival, we would dress for dinner at the most exclusive dinning room to be followed by a cabaret type show. After the show, staying the night was not required, and our driver would take anyone choosing to do so back to New York.

Bethany was quick to say she was staying the two nights. Margo was laughing when she said that, as an old woman, she would like to shock her adult grandchildren by disclosing that she paid for her last year of law school by being a whore for three nights. Both could not stop their thanks for the unbelievable gift they were receiving.

When our limo arrived, we were escorted to the Presidential Suite on the top floor of the sky tower. I noticed that we did not have to stop to check in. The suite in the New York hotel had been upscale. This was way beyond. Living room, dining room, three bedrooms, with three full and a one-half bathroom. The furniture would have fit nicely in the royal palace in London. All Bethany could say was "oh my God". Margo was the first to realize we had a butler on call for any service.

Dinner was as advertised. The cost of the silver and china would have paid for a small house. Seating capacity could not have been over forty. None of the menus showed any prices. The same

was true for the wine list. This dining room had to
be for the very wealthy or the big gamblers (the
high-rollers) that the casino offered extravagant
meals and wine as a complimentary service based on
their gaming play. All of the staff knew our host as
Mr. Fanucci.

The meal and wine were equal to the ambiance of
our surroundings. Our primary waiter demonstrated
his experience when, with a broad smile, he asked
the girls which chocolate dessert they would prefer.
We would have more drinks following dinner at the
show room.

The show was upbeat, several singers with a cast
of dancers, great costumes and a band reminiscent of
the old Lawrence Welk television productions.

Back in the suite, Nucci and Margo went directly
to a bedroom while Bethany and I stayed up to talk.
She had a lot of questions which I could understand.
I begged off for the evening, suggesting some cuddle
time, sleep, and a long walk in the morning when I
would answer her questions. It seemed a shame that
a third bedroom in all this luxury would go unused.

Following breakfast, Nucci would go to the poker

room. This was a thirty table facility where there was table-side dining. We would see him again when cocktail hour arrived. Margo headed for a morning around the pool to work on a tan. She would meet us for lunch. Bethany and I were off for a walk along the beautiful Thames river.

CHAPTER TWENTY-TWO

As we started along the banks of the beautiful river, Bethany took my hand, kissed my cheek, and said it was walk and talk time. My time to talk is what was meant.

I commenced with some family history. I was third-generation of Italian immigrants. My father had moved to the Bronx, married my mother, opened a neighborhood grocery, and raised two children. My sister was the college graduate while I left for the Army following high school. I was very proud that I entered and completed Special Forces training. The Army was to be my career.

My life changed when my father became ill and died soon thereafter. My mother could not manage alone. My sister had married, living out of state, so mother's finances and the grocery store were on my back. After taking a family hardship Army discharge, I returned to the Bronx to try to operate the grocery. It was just too late. The debt was too much and the business was loosing to the large chains. To save Mother from the debt, I burned the grocery building to collect the insurance proceeds. So now she should know that she had been sleeping with a criminal.

I must have looked very sad as Bethany took me in her arms in a strong embrace. Nothing was said as we stayed in each others arms for at least a full minute.

I said to Bethany that there was more. She held my hand as we walked slowly in the warm sunshine. I started back talking about life after the fire. I had to find a job, for my support, but also to help Mother who was left with only social security benefits. The South Bronx is a poor area. It is also a tough area where one can be robbed, injured or killed by just being in the wrong place. I had been a boxing champion as a teen, so I had some reputation as a tough guy. This led to me being approached with a job offer. I accepted to become engaged in the small loan business, the unlicensed loaning of money to poor people at illegally high interest rates. I was now a loan shark in an illegal business. She should recall that I told her a whore does not hurt people, but I am in a business that often does. These people need some means to have credit, but the high cost of borrowing is a killer to most of them.

Bethany started to speak when I said there was one other confession she should hear. I told of the time I was attacked in an attempted robbery at knife point. I was able to put the two down. However, I was cut and became so enraged that I took the knife to kill the defenseless young man. So she should see that she was walking with a man who has killed someone, burned a building, and was now in the business of illegal loans.

We stopped. Bethany told me she was walking with a man who was willing to take the chance of losing a relationship by being honest. From her teenage dates throughout all of college, she had never felt she would always hear the truth. She said she did not condone all I had done or was still doing, but she did understand necessity. Her focus in school was corporate law. Her plan was to join a law firm representing large corporate clients. She knew from her teachers that the corporate races for profits would often come down to breaking laws to get ahead. As their lawyer, she would have to decide her own ethics. She could not disclose their crimes. She could quit, look but not see, or become complicit. She would worry about that next year. Right now there was nothing about me that changed her wanting to continue our time together.

There were some very nice kisses and hugs as we returned along the river to meet Margo for lunch.

CHAPTER TWENTY-THREE

The number of restaurants and cafes in the hotel building was awesome. Any kind of food one could dream of was available. Bethany and Margo were insistent that we go Italian for me. I did not argue that I have eaten good Italian food since childhood and would have liked to try one of the other specialty venues. It was just nice they were trying to please me.

Margo had a fine morning at the pool. She had been asked to join several young women enjoying a Bloody Mary or two. All had husbands or boyfriends busy in the casinos. In response to their questions, Margo said simply she was with a male friend. One woman with ample bitch genes had said her answer must mean a married man. Margo had responded that the number of offers she received from men precluded checking on the marital status of each. Maybe Margo had her share of similar genes.

When lunch was completed, with two bottles of wine consumed, we all had a nap in mind. What we knew about dinner was to wear casual clothes, to be dressed and ready by seven o'clock, and to expect a surprise dinner. It was becoming quite clear that Nucci liked to provide the unexpected.

Nucci was back by six o'clock, time to have one quick drink before a shower for the evening. He was in a very good mood because the players at his table had more money than poker sense. He laughed when he refused to disclose the amount of his winnings or the specifics of the dinner arrangements.

At precisely seven o'clock there was a knock on our door. Led by our butler, a parade of dining room staff brought in a table with four chairs, four china and crystal place settings with silverware, and lace napkins. Our butler seated the girls, provided menus from one of the five-star restaurants, and opened chilled champagne. He would be in the hall just outside the door to take our orders or answer any questions. Nucci was handed some type of electronic device to call him in.

Nucci was in high spirits. I knew the pleasure of winning at poker, but I thought he was actually excited over the surprise dinner he had planned. The dinner was exceptional.

As we downed the champagne, he asked us to decide what we would like from the menu so that appropriate wine could be ordered. Questions arose, so our butler was called to go over the menu and to add any special dishes for the evening. It all looked so good, but finally our decisions were made. Nucci then took over to order several bottles of wine that he considered would enhance the food selections. He had quite a knowledge of very expensive wines.

The food arrived on silver trays balanced by four of the restaurant staff. Our butler brought the wines, opened the bottles, and had Nucci give a taste approval for the bottle to accompany the salad selections. When the main courses arrived, Nucci tasted the bottle to go with the dishes he and Margo had ordered, while I was to do the same for the bottle Bethany and I would share. I told Bethany later that I was totally faking when I approved the taste as I had no clue how to judge fine wine. My Italian family was much into wine, but never at such a price level.

Following a delicious main course (Bethany and I both had lobster), we moved to our balcony for dessert in the evening. This had the dual purpose of allowing an area where Nucci could have a favorite cigar without overwhelming his guests.

While we were enjoying the balcony, the hotel staff had completely cleaned the living room. We were living a lifestyle not shared by ordinary people. After dessert and more drinks, it was time for all to retire for the evening. Bethany and I decided to wait for the arrival of morning for sexual relations as we both were rather drunk.

The morning cuddled together was about as good as sex can be. My partner was a joy unlike any in my experience. Maybe the best part is that I could feel she really wanted to be with me. We both did not want the Mogehan Sun holiday to end.

Breakfast, which had been ordered by our butler, arrived by the time we had dressed. Eggs Benedict with hash brown potatoes would be a great start for the day. This was our first meal served without alcohol.

The ride back to the city was only me and the girls. Nucci had decided to have one more day at the poker table. We wished him luck, gave profuse thanks for the wonderful two days, and entered the limo for the drive back to New York.

I was pleased that Margo expressed her enjoyment of the trip. She said she would hope one day to find a rich man as nice to her as Nucci who was not married. While many, definitely her parents, would think she should be ashamed of this affair, she simply was not. She did add that she was not going to continue as a long-time partner to adultery even though the experience had been much fun.

Our driver went to the University in Manhattan before taking me to the Bronx. Bethany told me I was allowed three days to call her. If I failed to do so, she would call me. She was definitely going to have my call within her allowed time frame.

CHAPTER TWENTY-FOUR

My friendship with Nucci was solid. We talked by phone often, had lunch or dinner most weeks, including dinners at his home. His wife Rosa, was an attractive woman, very pleasant, good sense of humor, and also of Italian heritage. She had a good understanding of when to be present, but also when to leave the men to allow private conversation. She would say she doubted men wanted to be alone to discuss weather conditions. More likely gambling, drinking, sports, women and sex. I would joke with her that she might have omitted politics.

Her Italian cooking was to dream for. I almost made a mistake of saying it was better than we had at the Mohegan Sun. Nucci might have taken her there or maybe not. He could have told her where he was those two nights or maybe not.

Rosa would sometimes be invited to meet us for lunch. This was not often. I sensed she would always do everything she thought her husband wanted. Otherwise, she was content to stay at home. They had two children, a son and a daughter. The son was a freshman at Syracuse University. The daughter was a sophomore at an exclusive girls preparatory school in upstate New York. Rosa's favorite times were when the children were home from school.

She wanted to know about my social life. I had called Bethany during the three day deadline. We were together a lot. Nothing was being said about an exclusive relationship, although I was certain this was what existed. Rosa was adamant that Bethany should come with me for an Italian home cooked meal. Nucci assured me that this was no problem. I would caution Bethany not to mention being with Nucci before this dinner evening.

The dinner invitation was extended and accepted. Bethany's personality meshed well with Rosa's. Before the evening was over their conversations were for girls only. Nucci and I headed for the patio where his cigar could be enjoyed.

When the evening came to a conclusion, Rosa was bold enough to predict that Bethany and I would have a life together. She would even emphasize that marriage was far better than the current live together arrangements of many young people. She hoped

Bethany and I would join with her and Nucci
for a Catholic Church service.

Rosa was too smart not to know that her husband
had affairs. It took a strong woman to accept her
role as a wife married to a Mafia figure. I thought
she must care for Nucci, maybe loved him, but her
children and her church were the strong glue that
would hold everything together.

Bethany smiled when she said, should I want us
to live together, she was calling in Rosa to talk to me
about marriage.

CHAPTER TWENTY-FIVE

One day over lunch I was telling Nucci about a bad situation I was having with a loan collection. My partner had made a major error in judgment in making a one thousand dollar loan to a man who turned out to be a "gang-banger", a member of a small Bronx gang. Trying to collect could be a dangerous situation for me. I had to decide to go for a collection or absorb the loss.

Nucci stopped me. He asked that I allow him to go talk to the gang member. He said that he had a strong reputation for being able to convince people to follow his request after speaking with them. I saw no reason to turn him down. I gave him the name, and he was to follow up that afternoon.

Late that same afternoon Nucci called to tell me the debtor had agreed to pay the entire obligation including interest the next morning. That seemed pretty amazing. Early in the morning I followed up by going to the home of the gang-banger in a public housing unit. He handed me cash for the total due. His only comment was that he didn't know I was "connected".

When I called Nucci with my thanks he just replied that people have to understand failure to pay their debts can have consequences.

In a few days Nucci called to tell me it was time to have some fun. He gave me an address to meet him at nine o'clock Sunday morning. He would explain when I arrived.

The address was an ongoing construction site. There were two mostly completed floors of what appeared to be a several story building. There were numerous pieces of the contractor's heavy equipment on the property. Nucci was there with about a dozen other men. He told me to get on a backhoe with him. All of the equipment was started by some method that did not require keys. Mayhem followed. Bulldozers crashed into the sides of the partially complete building. Front-end loaders moved rubble that had fallen. In less that an hour the entire construction was nothing but a pile of brick, stone, pipe and wood. At that point everyone involved left the property, but not before sand was poured in the fuel tanks of every piece of equipment on site.

When I asked what was going on, Nucci told me the contractor that had made the low bid for this city building work was not using union employees. Being from upstate New York, the owner must not have understood that being a union bargained employer was important inside the Big Apple. I could hardly stop laughing as I agreed that a lesson should have been learned.

I followed the news accounts. The contractor abandoned the project. There was an ongoing dispute between the contractor and its insurance company over payment for the loss. The work to clear the site and to complete the city building was again put out for bid. This time only union employee companies submitted bids.

CHAPTER TWENTY-SIX

The next time I was with Nucci was for afternoon beers at the same bar where he first met Bethany and Margo. Bethany was to join us later after class for pizza. Rosa was also coming to join the group. It was unusual for her to come to a bar. We both thought it was because of her liking for Bethany.

Nucci and I usually engaged in "guy talk", sports, politics, gambling, drinking and women, not in any particular order. This afternoon was different. Nucci wanted me to listen while he talked. I obliged.

He had not directly told me he was involved in the Mafia. That was now to come. He started by naming the five New York Mafia "families", Bonanno, Colombo, Gambino, Genovese, and Lucchese. Together, all of New York City was divided into Mafia controlled areas or districts. The families were in direct competition in criminal activity but, in modern times, did not ordinarily engage in warfare against each other. There had been a "hit" every few years over area control.

He would not tell me the name of his family, only that he was very high in the organization. Because of his rank, he could stay away from the notorious crimes of drugs, gambling, and prostitution. His area was unions, which explained the construction demolition I had been invited to attend. Why the Mafia attention to unions? This was because union control meant control of the union membership pension funds. Many millions were involved which could be skimmed by having control.

We ordered another beer as Nucci continued. In the United States, a "made man" is a fully initiated member of the Mafia. Originally, when the Mafia moved into America, an inductee was required to be a male of full Sicilian descent. This requirement was later modified to include males of full Italian descent, and even later to males of one-half Italian descent through their father's lineage. The one-half Italian was later deleted. My full Italian heritage would make me eligible if sponsored by Nucci.

An "associate" could serve in the Mafia, but only a "made man" could rise through the ranks of soldier to caporegime, consigliere, underboss, and boss. Other common names for members included "man of honor", "one of us", "friend of ours", "goodfella", and "wise guy". The news media likes the term "Mafioso" which is a phrase not used by Mafia members.

Nucci said he would sponsor me if I wanted to join his Mafia family. In his family the "books were open" meaning new members could be accepted. He went on to say, for reasons he would not then detail, that his thoughts were I would be best served by staying away from being a member.

For a reason I would soon know, Nucci changed subjects to my Special Forces training in the use of a rifle. I replied that I had excelled. My ranking in rifle accuracy was first among all of the candidates. I was given special training to be a sniper when necessary.

Then he changed the conversation to a member of the New York Prosecutor's Office. Vincent "Vinny" Vigliano had announced he was a candidate for Mayor of New York in the upcoming election. His platform was that only he had the experience as a prosecutor to rid the city of organized crime. If elected, he would go around the generally corrupt city police force by asking for the National Guard to be brought in to take charge. Vinny was seeking publicity that would make him mayor, then on to the governor's office, with ambitions to become president. Vinny needed to be killed. A plan was already in place.

I was becoming a little confused where Nucci was going. There was a slight interruption for a bathroom break followed by our next beer. Then he continued.

Vinny was going to make an opening campaign speech in Central Park the next Saturday. A platform to speak from was under construction. Laser measurement showed that the platform was five hundred twenty yards from a second floor window of an empty warehouse accessible to the Mafia. A rifle with sight set for this exact distance was being transported to New York.

Only one security camera would be operational, the one covering the back door entrance. A man with a portion of his face and hands exposed would enter through the door carrying the rifle. The exposed skin would show him to be a black man. When the speech started, the timing would have to be exact. The shooter would have only one shot. Immediately after firing, the black man would run out the back door carrying the rifle, throw the rifle into the back seat of a waiting car, and walk away. The security camera would be turned off as the shooter exits the building.

If all goes well, the police will be looking for a black man as the killer. This black man has palsy that would render him unable to make such a rifle shot. Saying all bases had been covered, Nucci asked if I would be willing to be the shooter, then told me not to answer yet.

He went on by telling me that, before being inducted, a potential "made man", is required to carry out a contract killing. Traditionally, this was to show loyalty. In modern times, it serves to show that one is not an undercover law enforcement agent trying to infiltrate the Mafia. He could cause an expedited process whereby the Vinny murder would cover my contract killing requirement.

I was now very confused. I could not decide what Nucci wanted. He had earlier said he would not recommend the Mafia for me. He finally brought all that he had been saying into a tight bundle. There were two reasons he felt I would be better off outside the Mafia. First and foremost,

131

being at the bottom, a soldier must carry out orders. I could be forced into drug dealing which he considered the worst of all the crimes. Second, my required contract killing would be without money compensation. If I am hired to kill Vinny, the compensation has been set at one hundred thousand dollars in cash. While I was making a nice living, that much money could be used to make my mother's last years better.

So now, just before Bethany and Rosa arrived, Nucci said to answer his question about being the shooter by the next morning.

CHAPTER TWENTY-SEVEN

Bethany arrived at the bar with Rosa just slightly behind. Bethany was ready for alcohol as she had taken a difficult law school examination earlier in the afternoon. The test subject was Securities Law. She thought she had done well (as she had all through law school, near the top of her class). When I inquired about the subject matter, she laughed as she answered with her conclusion that most of the big players on Wall Street should be in jail.

Rosa embraced Bethany, spoke to me, and then greeted her husband. She commented that the bar decor could use some work. Her drink choice was a glass of nice Italian red that would go well with pizza. Bethany had ordered a vodka martini made with Absolut Citron, two olives, and a lime twist. Nucci and I continued with our choice of beer.

Rosa commented how pleased she was that Bethany was my date for the evening. She made sure I was aware of my good fortune. Most of the following conversation was between the two females. This was good with me as I was never among the best at social conversations.

At the time to order pizza everyone decided wine should be the alcohol choice. Bethany and I agreed on a choice of pizza to be split. Rosa and Nucci each ordered their own, Rosa with tomatoes and peppers while Nucci went with Italian sausage and onions. I thought this bar pizza was as good as those ordered for delivery from the name competitors.

While Rosa went to the ladies room, Bethany whispered to me that she had arranged for Margo to sleep elsewhere so I could join her in the dormitory for a "sleep over". She said there was a second toothbrush by her sink. With her big smile she told me she could not remember how many men had used the brush.

I was really fond of Bethany. She was beautiful, smart, with an outgoing personality, and sometimes sassy. She had no problem being the one to arrange for sex later in the evening. Not a shy girl.

I had asked the bartender for the food and drink bill. Rosa intervened. She would pay the bill to see how much we guys had to drink. Nucci just smiled at her.

It was easy to take the subway to Bethany's dorm. The days of separate dorms for males and females had mostly passed. The rooms were usually staggered, male next to female, with large separate toilet and shower rooms down each hall. Each room had two single beds which could be pulled together to accommodate close relationships.

I enjoyed the usual great sex. We both slept soundly until Bethany's alarm interrupted to bring in the morning. She was off to class while I had a major decision to make.

CHAPTER TWENTY-EIGHT

It is often easy for someone to rationalize how something so wrong can be right when it has a great personal benefit. Such was my situation. Murder is wrong by biblical, legal, and moral standards. But Vinny was to be killed. The murder would happen. The only question was what person would pull the trigger. Accepting the hit would net me one hundred thousand dollars. This money would allow my mother to be secure in her last years. I called Nucci to express agreement that I would be his man.

We met for hours to discuss every small detail. No mistake could be allowed. There was a small change. The only security camera in operation at the warehouse would stay on continually. This way investigators would not find a gap in coverage. The black man with the rifle would enter and leave through the door with the camera. A side entry would be available for me to enter the building and leave the same way.

I entered the warehouse at the designated time on the morning of Vinny's speech. My clothing included gloves. The man with the rifle was already there. I set up at the window to await Vinny's appearance. As his speech commenced, I took careful aim viewing only his chest. I did not want to see his face. There was a well practiced squeeze of the trigger. The bullet went through his chest into the heart. His life was ended. My murder was complete.

I handed the rifle to the black man who went out the door with the camera. My exit was through the side door. As arranged by Nucci, I went to a house a few blocks away. A man awaited with an entire new set of clothes including boxer shorts, socks and shoes. All of my clothes were burned in an outdoor fire pit. I was in and out in less than five minutes.

I walked along a prescribed route that avoided the dozens of police and emergency vehicles with sirens screaming. My walking was for about an hour. I wanted to be a long distance from the warehouse before getting on public transportation.

The television news was only about the shooting. It had taken the police some five minutes to determine the shot came from the warehouse. I had been out in less than one minute as had the black man. It was a few hours until the security camera video was all over the news. As Nucci had calculated, there was no mention of a Mafia kill. A black person with the heritage requirement to be in the Mafia would be rare. Also, Vinny had been accused of being abusive in prosecutions of members of the black community in the city.

When we next met, Nucci brought me a package containing one hundred thousand dollars in one hundred dollar bills. He joked with his thought that I had best not deposit the money with my bank.

CHAPTER TWENTY-NINE

I really wanted to get away from what I had done for at least a few days. Bethany solved this for me. Having finished a paper early, she had a week off from school classes. She asked me to fly to Iowa for a short visit with her family. This would be followed by renting a car to drive to a friend's cabin in the Black Hills near Deadwood, South Dakota.

I was not sure of the location of Iowa, had no clue as to South Dakota, and was somewhat apprehensive about meeting her family. None of this made any difference. I wanted to be away from New York and with Bethany. I was going.

We took a flight into Aims, Iowa where Bethany had attended college at Iowa State. She had to handle the car rental as I had never acquired a driver's license. I had driven military vehicles only. My family had never owned a car. Her family lived in Huxley, a town of about four thousand located ten miles from Aims.

We arrived at a small frame house on a quiet

street just within the town limits. I had concern with questions being posed about my occupation. Bethany assured me her parents were not business sophisticated. I should just say I was employed by a loan company. The house had three bedrooms. Her brother was now away in a junior college, so I would have his room. Bethany would be in the room with her sister as had been the situation growing up. She was not yet willing to ask to sleep with me in her parent's home.

We had a nice visit. Her parents were pleasant, easy to talk to. Especially her father who wanted to know all about my Special Forces training. He had served for several years in the Marines. Her sister had matured into a pleasant young lady one year away from college. Bethany had lied to her parents about the expense of her final year in law school. She told them that an extra scholarship came through along with another student loan.

The next day we drove into Aims to tour the Iowa State campus before our road trip to the Black Hills of South Dakota. Our drive would be to Sioux Falls, South Dakota before stopping for lunch. Then more than five hours on Interstate 90 West to a turn into the hills just above Deadwood. At the turn, we bought supplies for the four days and three nights at the cabin. This would be quite an experience for a city boy.

To call what we found on arrival a cabin was right on point. It was basically a one-room wood structure with an attached bathroom. It did have electricity and running water. The one large room had a sofa and two chairs in the living area, a kitchen with dining table, and a double bed. The sofa would pull out into another bed. There were a lot of stuffed animals serving as wall decorations. Heat was available by two large space heaters.

We were tired from the drive, more so Bethany, who was our sole driver. I could have operated the car, but prudence was to avoid driving without a license.

We unloaded the car together. Looking at each other, no talking was necessary for our decision to try out the bed before getting drunk while cooking dinner.

Bethany opened the wine. I had volunteered to use my limited skills to cook our first meal of pasta with Italian red sauce. The meal was a success. At least it seemed to be good after we had consumed two bottles of wine.

This time we got in the bed with a purpose of sleep. The next day would be started with breakfast followed by a drive down to the famous town of Deadwood. I had read a book Bethany brought for me on the airplane flight to Aims. It was a detailed history of the town. I had not previously known of this town, but had some vague memory of the names Wyatt Earp, Calamity Jane and Wild Bill Hickok.

I learned that Deadwood was settled in the Black Hills Gold Rush days of the nineteenth century. It was named for the dead trees found in its gulch.

The land had actually been granted to the Lakota Indians by a treaty with the United States in 1868. The situation changed when Colonel George Armstrong Custer led an expedition that discovered the Black Hills gold in 1874. Gold hunting miners stormed into the territory by the thousands. This created the new and lawless town of Deadwood.

Over breakfast, and on the drive down, I told Bethany of the history I had read. She listened with an appearance of interest. I suspected she knew everything I had read and was just happy to have me pleased with our trip together. The trip was a bonus. Spending time with Bethany made me happy.

With thousands seeking the spoils of gold, gamblers, whores, and saloon operators joined the flood of miners. The first wagon train of supplies brought several of the madames who provided prostitutes in high demand by the miners. History has that Madame Dora DuFram became the most profitable brothel owner in Deadwood.

When we arrived in Deadwood, I told Bethany I first wanted to see the saloon where Wild Bill Hickok was murdered. As a child, I had only heard the name when kids played Cowboys and Indians. From the history book, I now knew Hickok was not only a famous gunfighter, but an avid poker player. Poker peaked my interest. My choice of a first stop was the building reputed to be the original location of the Nuttal & Mann's saloon.

Wild Bill was shot in the back while playing poker by a man named Jack McCall. The five card poker hand held by Hickok when he was murdered contained two aces, two eights, and a queen. In poker circles to this day, a hand containing two aces and two eights is called "deadman's hand".

McCall had entered the saloon where the poker game was held, had a drink at the bar, and walked over to the table to shoot Hickok in the back of his head. There were no judges or courts in this lawless territory. A group of miners decided they would hold a trial for McCall who claimed he had killed Wild Bill to avenge the killing of his brother. This claim was not true, but avenging a family death was considered at that time as justification for retaliation. McCall was found not guilty.

Of further interest to me, McCall went around the Dakota's bragging that he was the man who killed the great gunfighter. A United States Marshall heard this bragging, arrested him, and a second trial was allowed. The first trial was ruled invalid because it took place in Indian territory. This time, he was convicted and hanged.

When panning for gold was replaced, by the large mines, most of those who had panned moved on to different territory.

Deadwood was not changed much over the years, although it had several major fires. Each time there was rebuilding that brought the town to the small tourist attraction that it remains to this day.

CHAPTER THIRTY

After our day in Deadwood, Bethany and I were back at the cabin for our evening and remaining two days. Life in the Black Hills could not be more different from that in New York. With Bethany, and being far away from my act of murder, I would have been content to stay for weeks, possibly a lot longer.

Surrounding our cabin were numerous trails for hiking, horseback riding, and mountain biking. I never had a bike. I would see the New York police riding horses, but I never was on one, nor did I have any desire to do so. My Iowa girl was quick to tease me about the confines of the large city.

That evening was her turn to prepare our meal. She made a vegetable and cheese casserole that could have been a primary main course dish in a high-end restaurant. I did a good job of opening the wine. After dinner, we sat on the sofa, listening to sounds of animals and birds, holding hands while looking at each other. For the first time, we both spoke of being in love.

Deep down, I was very afraid this could not last. She had a promising career ahead while I had become a true criminal. I would savor every moment with her.

With horses and bikes out of the equation, the next morning brought hiking the trails. Bethany used the gym at her school to stay in good physical shape. I had continued to use boxing as a means of exercise. We could handle the long trail over to the Deer Mountain ski area. Clean air, some beautiful lakes, trees and flowers, were a really good experience for me. Except for central park, I normally saw a lot of brick and concrete.

The remainder of our time was spent hiking, drinking, and eating, accompanied by a lot of sex. Not just casual sex, but the kind between a couple truly in love.

I could understand how one could live happily in the Black Hills. Everyone knows it is said that all good things must come to an end. Our time ran out. We drove back to Aims, turned in the rental car, and boarded our airplane back to the big city.

I thought a lot about telling Bethany I was the

one who murdered Vinny. Total honesty was so important to her. This time it was just too much. I had to live with one huge secret.

Back in the city, we continued as a steady item. I was watching the calendar carefully as the weeks moved closer to Bethany's law school graduation. Decisions I did not want to make were closing in.

CHAPTER THIRTY-ONE

Being absent for one week did not cause a disruption in my loan collection business. There had been no problems that could not wait. I had a thought that Nucci's talk with the gang-banger had gotten attention in the South Bronx. Perhaps word was out that we had means to enforce payment of all of our loans.

Speaking of Nucci, I got a strange phone call from him. He wanted me to read several articles that would be delivered. I was not to mention the articles to anyone including Bethany. We would get together later for discussion over a couple of beers.

The envelope from Nucci was left at my door. The subject was the United States Central Intelligence Agency (the CIA). The articles taken together asserted that within the huge, vast, global agency is an obscure department which is a part of a larger Division. This small, very secret group of agents is known inside the CIA as the "**KILL SQUAD**". These agents, acting on direct order and authority of the President of the United States, are assassins. Their victims are those persons considered a threat to the national security of the United States.

Following an embarrassing United States Senate investigation in the early 1970's which disclosed the scale of these CIA operations, then President Gerald Ford signed in 1976 an executive order that no U.S. Government employee shall engage in, or conspire in, political assassination.

The impact of the order by President Ford was zero. The top level of U.S. Government after Ford wanted to continue their power to kill those they considered enemies of the state. The terminology was simply changed from assassination to targeted killings.

Of the more than twenty thousand agents of the CIA spy organization, members of the "Kill Squad" are the most glamorous. Being subject only to orders of the President, they prepare and travel the globe to carry out assignments to kill, now called targeted killings.

There are special laws on the books to protect the secrets of the "Kill Squad". Any agent or former agent who makes a disclosure can be immediately taken into custody without a warrant, held for an indefinite time, and brought to a secret trial.

My assigned reading went on to raise long-standing questions of whether those in power had used the CIA to rid themselves of politically embarrassing persons who were never a threat to national security.

The famous beauty, movie actress and star, Marilyn Monroe, was found in a bed of her fashionable home in California, nude and dead by overdose of barbiturates. There had been rumors of her affair with President John F. Kennedy, and also that his brother, Senator Robert Kennedy, had found her bedroom inviting. The most persistent rumor following the death was that Kennedy friends in the CIA had injected her with the lethal dose of drugs to protect the Kennedy brothers from scandal.

It was asserted that Robert Kennedy was at the Monroe home the day prior to her death. Conjecture was that he was trying to break off the relationships.

The Los Angeles Police homicide investigator, first police officer on the scene, stated his opinion that she was murdered with needle injection by someone she knew and trusted. The Deputy Coroner who signed the death certificate said later that he did so under duress.

There was also an issue of Marilyn's dairy, the so-called "red" diary. She was known to keep this diary which was never found after her death. There was much contention that this book named a lot of national figures including both Kennedys and certain San Diego Mafia members.

Much later, after President Bill Clinton took office, the "Clinton Body Count" rumors began. The start may have been when Deputy White House council Vincent Foster was found dead from an apparent self-inflicted gun shot wound to the head in Fort Marcy Park in Virginia in 1993. Though his death was ruled a suicide, it remains a subject of conspiracy theories that Bill and Hillary Clinton had him murdered for knowing too much.

Later, conspiracy theorists constructed a long list of suspicious deaths (the body count) of persons that had some association with Bill and Hillary.

I thought these articles were very interesting. I

would have to wait for Nucci to explain why they were directed to me.

CHAPTER THIRTY-TWO

Over a few beers, Nucci told me of his friendship with an agent of the CIA that he would not name. While the agency maintained the small group of assassins I had read about, current policy was to recruit, train and employ former military specialists, such as Army Special Forces, to be "off the books" assassins. These men and women have worked for the CIA, but all records as to them have been kept top secret. This created more assassins totally unknown to the vast networks of foreign spy agencies who have been able to identify some of the long-time agents.

Nucci observes and understands much that he has not been directly told. He continued, that he knew that Bethany wanted us to be married. He realized that I was aware that she could not have employment in prominent law firms if married to a known loan shark. I had to be torn between wanting her for myself and not wanting to be the cause of the loss of her promising legal career.

I should meet with his CIA friend. If I was

accepted into this type of covert activity and performed well for an agreed number of "kills", I would be eligible to "retire" from CIA service. Further, my record would show that I had served in CIA employment since I was discharged from the military. This Division of the agency takes very good care of its employees. Cleansing my past would be no problem. I could marry Bethany with a record of outstanding military duty followed by continued service to our country in the CIA.

I agreed to meet with this government agent. It was only the next day that I received a call. We would have the meeting on a bench in Central Park. I was to wear a red shirt and a New York Yankees baseball cap. He would be dressed the same.

When I arrived in the park, my contact was seated on the bench dressed as agreed. He said I would never know his name. To me, he would be "Contact Red".

He first explained that everything that was said between us, this day and every time hereafter, would not just be confidential, it could not be disclosed forever. He went on that any violation, even years later, would subject me to arrest and trial to be held in secret. Actually, rather than an arrest, it was more likely I would be found dead. I did not think Contact Red was the type to be joking.

The identities of assassins housed within the offices of the CIA were in constant danger of exposure. Certainly the worldwide spy networks were always working toward this end. Another problem had arisen with the introduction of the "whistleblower", usually a disgruntled employee, who uses access to confidential records to have his "fifteen minutes of fame" by making disclosures to the news media. All of this had led to engaging qualified individuals outside the CIA offices (off the books) as additional assassins.

On preliminary information, I seemed to meet the agency's qualifications. My special forces service made obvious that I had been trained to kill. My Italian heritage would have me less obvious as being an American in foreign countries. It was also important that I was not married. Wives expect to know where their husband are, together with the details of their employment. A wife of CIA agents engaged in kills cannot have this information.

Contact Red asked if I would be willing to kill any person or persons designated by the CIA. I could easily answer this. There seemed to be no difference from killing in an army battle situation. In both cases the kills are of enemies of the United States.

Contact Red seemed satisfied. He wanted a few days to check my entire background. If a contract was to be offered, he would give me answers to all questions before I would be asked to make a decision. Another caution about secrecy, and he was gone.

CHAPTER THIRTY-THREE

I received a call from Bethany. Her grades were so good in the last semester she had been relieved of the usual final examinations. She would graduate in a little over two weeks. The number of job interviews she had been offered was a surprise to her. New York was certainly a potential, but the most prestigious firm in contact was one of the several largest in Boston. It was a "blue-blood" old Boston firm with primarily large corporate clients in Massachusetts and extending into New York.

She wanted my promise to be with her at graduation. Her family just did not have extra money for travel and the expense of New York. I would have gone without a request.

She knew I would come to graduation. She did want me to know everything going on, why she would be so busy with interviews until then. But now, the more important reason for her call. She wanted a serious conversation with me about our future together. We agreed to the evening of graduation for celebration, spending that night together, with the next day for candid and truthful talk.

I was very glad to hear from Contact Red. I needed to know the details of any offer that was forthcoming. A decision should be made before I could talk about the future with Bethany. We met again on the same park bench in the same attire.

I first wanted an answer as to whether the targeted killings were actually legal by law. The reply was that the National Security Act authorized covert actions. A Pentagon study concluded that the CIA should have exclusive control of such actions.

Next, I wanted to have information about training. Contact Red told me there would be about one month of concentrated training. After completion of this training, each job assignment would have more training specific to the target. I would work with seasoned agents as to means to get into position for the kill. Sometimes getting close to the target might take weeks in a foreign country. Every kill was different.

Following covert action an escape must be in the plan. Sometimes this could be as simple as walking away. Other situations might require assistance from locals willing to help the United States.

Then there was the potential of failure with a resulting capture by enemy combatants. I would have to decide to accept capture, with likely torture, or decide that death was a better decision. I would always have a suicide poison available.

Contact Red then spoke of weapons. I would be familiar with the military type, but not so with others, especially the poisons. One new weaponry was the drone. I would have to be able to operate all sizes carrying various weapons.

Back to poisons, the CIA would never admit to the use of poison, not even to the top level of government. In 1969, then-President Richard Nixon announced the United States would never engage in germ warfare and ordered the destruction of our stockpile of bacteriological weapons. There was a small exception (used to a large extent) that toxins needed for defensive research could be maintained.

Russia had long been noted for the use of poison against defectors to other countries and political enemies. There would be no need for me to have information as to poison use by the CIA. The stock answer was that it had never happened.

Contact Red had a slight smile (the first sign of any emotion) as he gave me a poison background for my education only.

Project Naomi was the code name for the development of poisons and incapacitating agents by the CIA. Somehow the records of these developments disappeared when the U.S. Senate requested the information during its investigations in the 1970's.

The most deadly poison known to have been developed by the CIA was a shellfish toxin, named saxitoxin, with no known antidote, which could kill thousands of people. Saxitoxin, distilled from a particular clam, was similar to a toxin made by the Japanese from puffer fish. There was also a very deadly poison made from the venom of a cobra, strychnine, cyanide pills, and BZ, a chemical that attacks the central nervous system.

While never actually used, I would be trained with a pistol-sized electric gun capable of firing poison pellets without any sound. The gun is noted to be accurate to two hundred fifty feet. Similarly, I would learn how to use a cane and an umbrella, both with poison in the tip.

Turning to questions of compensation, I was informed that pay would vary with circumstances, but that I would be very pleased with the amounts. Since I would not be on the published CIA payroll, my funds would come from "off the record" money that did not have to be accounted for. There was a lot of this type money authorized by congress for the agency. If asked by congressional auditors, the usual answer was such was needed to acquire necessary information through bribes of foreign officials. I would have credit cards when needed, and my money would be deposited into my account in an offshore bank.

My final question was to timing. Could I wait to start until after Bethany's graduation? With an affirmative answer, I was ready to begin a new career with the CIA.

CHAPTER THIRTY-FOUR

On law school graduation day I was surprised to see Nucci and Rosa join the large audience. He can be full of surprises, but I suspected Rosa was the driving force in their attendance.

On the graduation stage, Bethany was beautiful. Her blonde hair accented her blue eyes. Her face was bright with the usual smile, sometimes happy, sometimes mischievous. I was truly, more and more, in love.

At the conclusion of the ceremonies, I was standing with Nucci and Rosa. There was a moment of panic as Bethany and Margo walked toward us. No problem. Bethany smoothly introduced Margo to Nucci and Rosa as her roommate and best friend. After some polite conversation, Margo left our group to join her parents.

Rosa handed Bethany an envelope. It contained a gift certificate for dinner that night at an exclusive French restaurant on the top floor of a building overlooking Central Park. I had only heard of this restaurant, never thinking of dining in New York's most expensive dining venue. We would be in the company of the very wealthy.

We went to Bethany's dorm room to dress for the evening. Margo was staying at a hotel with her parents so the room was ours alone until the next day. While my dinner companion had a dress appropriate for such an evening, I was somewhat concerned that my slacks and sport coat might not be sufficient. I did not have a necktie.

Arriving at the seven o'clock designated time, I presented the certificate. The very polite young lady seated us at a prime table for two with an outstanding view. Nucci and Rosa had some obvious influence.

The menu offered only two meals changed by the chef daily. We both selected the same choice. After our selection, our waiter announced that our host had ordered wine to accompany our meal. Nucci was not going to leave me to stumble through a wine decision. I had looked at the wine list which was as limited as the meals available. Mentally adding the meals, wine, and normal tip, I calculated that the graduation gift exceeded fourteen hundred dollars.

Through the evening and back at the dorm, we had observed our decision to wait until the next morning to discuss our future together. We would dress for the school coffee shop to have our serious conversation. Staying in bed to talk most likely would not work as bed-talk often turned into other activity.

CHAPTER THIRTY-FIVE

We found a quiet corner table in the coffee shop. Bethany commenced by telling me her law office employment opportunities to date. While she had several New York small firm offers with two interviews to come, she was most excited to talk about her interview and offer from certainly one of the largest, most prestigious, firms in Boston. Their clients were corporations, large businesses, governments, and wealthy individuals. The starting salary offered was far better than she had imagined. The office recruiter was upfront about expectations. Each associate hired was expected to work to bill clients for seventy to eighty hours each week. The long hours of such work would last for a period of five years. After that time an associate would be made a partner in the firm or be asked to resign if not found to be partnership quality.

She then continued to tell me what she wanted for the future. This was so important and emotional that I can recite verbatim for you today every word that she said: "I love you Anthony. I want you to be my husband for ever and ever. You can come to Boston with me. I can work in New York, even in the Bronx. We can move to Iowa. I just want you. So, your brazen girlfriend is asking you to marry her. You can now speak."

I had difficulty speaking. I stammered in saying how much love I had for her. But now I had to escape emotion to move to reality.

The Boston firm that was so large would not accept her marriage to a known loan shark. It was doubtful any of the New York firms would be different. When an associate lawyer contemplates marriage, one can be assured that the firm protects its interest by investigation.

Now I moved to my important news. I then told her that I was taking employment with a United States government agency. While my job would be a national security matter, my record in a few years would be that I had served in the Army Special Forces with distinction, followed by U.S. Government service with the CIA that must always remain secret. If anyone questioned my time in the loan business, the answer would be that everything I did after the army was part of my secret career. In only a few years my record would be clean. Not only clean, but beyond scrutiny.

I would be leaving for training in a week. After that, I would be home some between missions that could last weeks or months. I had been promised no more than five assignments, maybe over three or four years, before I would received an employment discharge with a glowing report of service vital to our country. It could even be as little time as two or three years, only a maximum of five assignments.

I wanted marriage more than anything in life, but I also wanted her to have the legal career she had worked so long for. If we could only wait, continue to be together when we could, we would have years thereafter as a respectable couple. We would no longer be burdened by my past.

I had tried to follow her expressions as I talked. Could I have just ended the only real love relationship in my existence?

She looked at me for a time before commencing to speak. "Not only have I proposed marriage, I have now also been turned down. The burden for any future proposal has shifted to you. I am going to take the Boston employment. I am only twenty-five years old, so the five years as an associate will take me to thirty. I am giving you those five years to ask me to marry you. Fail that and I will move on."

"I hope we can be together often. In Boston I will be busy, but alone. I am not bashful about noting that I attract men. I expect to have a lot of offers of companionship. When you are away, I am not going to sit at home in the small amount of time I will not be working. I will go out with other men."

Then her impish smile appeared. "If I find a Boston man who is better in bed than you, I reserve the right to revoke your five years. Asshole!"

Thus was the beginning of the new era of our lives together. The train ride from Boston to New York was not long. Anytime I was home when she had time off from work was together time. We were careful when I was in Boston not to be seen as a couple. She did not need to be trying to explain her relations with me.

CHAPTER THIRTY-SIX

The training for my new venture was in a secure area of a military base reserved for the CIA. The first part was similar to army basic training. Get in physical shape, stay in physical shape.

The first part of weapons use was military-style, but with focus on pistols and long-range rifle fire. Use of explosives was far more extensive. There were a number of types beyond the military hand grenades and dynamite. I learned of timed explosives, small devices that could be hidden in offices or hotel rooms, and smoke generating bombs for diversion.

The drone training was extensive. I first had to learn how to fly all sizes. Then we got into the complexity of radar, camera vision, lasers, and use of information from ground observers to guide a drone attack. The drone operator had to know the range of the explosives carried to plan attack distance from the target. The learning was time consuming.

We were taught to throw a knife to a target. This was difficult because there was no standard-size weapon an operative would carry. Weight and size created so much variation in how a throw might hit the intended target. More important to knife usage was knowing the vital areas of the human body. The kill had to be quick and often silent.

The last of the weapons training involved those that could be used to assassinate with poison. I thought this to be quite interesting as Contact Red had given assurance (albeit with a slight smile) that the CIA did not possess any poison to use in a kill.

The most interesting weapon was the electric gun that could fire a very small poison missile to a maximum range of about two hundred fifty feet. Then there was the cane and the umbrella, each with a place for poison in the point, with a hidden trigger to pull after aiming. These were very short range, but they appeared to me to have a place in a surprise attack.

The final training was with actual operatives, past and present, who could give pointers such as infiltration, timing, choice of weapon, etc. While their points would help, it was obvious to me that an ultimate attack would be up to my best judgment.

    With training complete, I returned to the Bronx to await an assignment call from Contact Red. I did not have to wait long.

CHAPTER THIRTY-SEVEN

Mother's health had deteriorated to a point where I had moved her to a long-term care facility. I was not certain she knew where she was, but I was confident she was comfortable. I had to engage my sister to care for mother's needs during absences for my CIA employment. Anna was naturally curious about my mysterious employment. I managed to persuade her that I simply could not explain. She would just have to accept the situation and know there would be weeks, even months, when I could not be contacted.

Bethany had taken the Massachusetts and New York Bar examinations. As expected, she had passed both. Her work as a lawyer in Boston had commenced. Her small apartment was in a good and safe location away from the restaurants and bars. I could visit without other lawyers and law office workers asking questions about her New York friend.

She was as busy as had been contemplated, but had a little time to accept a few of the many social invitations. Bethany enjoyed teasing me as to the many attractive young business executives in Boston whom she described as rich and hot.

I had just returned to the Bronx from a Saturday night stay-over in Boston when my call came. I was to meet Contact Red for instructions as to my first assignment.

There was a Saudi Prince that had become a significant problem to the United States. Prince Abdul was high ranking in the Saudi Arabian ruling family. The Prince had become an advocate of a Saudi alignment with the Chinese government. After a disagreement with our Secretary of State, he was pushing to reduce relations with the U.S. Saudi Arabia was particularly important to the CIA as a base to intercede in terrorists operations in the Middle East. Matters had reached a point where the order was to eliminate the Prince.

I had been selected because of an unlikely common interest. The Prince was an avid poker player. Approximately once each month he sailed his yacht to Monte Carlo, Monaco to play high-stakes Texas Holdem at the Casino De Monte Carlo. His usual stay was five to seven days.

We had only a general plan for assassination. I could well expect to spend months getting the right moment for the kill. It was of monumental importance that the Saudi murder not be tied to the United States.

Initially I would fly to Nice, France. A rental car drive (using my furnished fake drivers license) was about thirty minutes to the town or small city of Menton, France, a seaside resort located between Monaco and Italy, where the Alps plunge into the shores of the Mediterranean. I would reside in Menton which was only a short train ride to Monte Carlo. This arrangement was better for keeping a low profile than living long-term in Monaco.

I found Menton to be an attractive small city. Due to a micro-climate that tends towards the sub-tropics, Menton is a gardener's paradise. The Fontana Rosa Garden was created in 1922 by a politician and writer to produce a memento of his native Valencia. The Maria Serena Garden, located near the Italian border in a quarter called "la petite Afrique" (little Africa), had a reputation for the mildest climate in France.

Although a tourist community, I was able to find

a monthly rental at a reasonable rent. It was interesting to me that I was furnished several credit cards without being informed of any budget. I was given twenty-five thousand Euros to use at the casino poker tables.

My local contact was working as a gardener at the Fontana Rosa Garden. He was a CIA operative who would obtain anything I should need to carry out my job.

I took the train to Monaco to learn about the Monte Carlo Casino, the surrounding area of the city, and the harbor where the Prince's yacht would be anchored upon arrival.

The casino was itself a wonder in opulence. I had been to Las Vegas. There was nothing in Vegas to compare with Monte Carlo. Monaco is noted to have more resident millionaires per person than any other city in the world. This facility was built to cater to the rich and famous.

The Hotel De Paris and the Cafe De Paris were almost as impressive. In fact, the entire city was unlike any I had known. Nowhere was the poverty of the South Bronx.

I went back to the casino to view the poker room. As expected, it was large with numerous tables in the main area. Off to the side were three private areas for higher limit games. Glass dividers allowed view of the players from outside these areas. I would likely first see the Prince in one of these rooms. I spoke to the room manager about playing in the higher limit games. If there were usual players wanting seats, they would have first priority, and otherwise I would be welcome. That is, unless the request for a seat was from a known celebrity. Celebrity in Monte Carlo had some privileges. I assumed the Prince was in the celebrity category.

I slipped into an elevator to see the residence floors of the hotel. As I suspected, there was extensive coverage by security cameras. Any activity in the halls would be recorded. The regular elevators did not go to the suites on the top two levels. Access to the Prince in his hotel room would be unlikely.

I had to assume my every move in the hotel and casino was within camera view. It might be days before the Prince would come so I did not need to rush anything. It would be normal for a visitor to be in Monte Carlo to gamble. I went to the poker tables for the remainder of this day.

It seemed to me that a person living in Menton might go to gamble every few days. That would be my normal routine to appear as a tourist in the French Riviera with some appetite for gambling.

My tourist cover next took a route to the seaside to enjoy a day in the sun. My white skin could use some tanning. Later this day I went to the collection of citrus trees of the Palais Carnoles, Europes largest collection of such trees enriched by the Prince's vegetable garden, the "Jardin remarkable" (remarkable garden).

My local contact would advise of news that our Prince was on his yacht, so I decided to explore my Italian roots by a visit to Ventimiglia, Italy, just across the border on a short train ride. This town was well known for a weekly street market. I had been warned that the some five hundred vendors operating out of stalls were selling mostly cheap goods.

An exception to the poor quality was the cashmere clothing, very expensive, but such as would be found in Paris. There was a sweater that would be a nice fit on Bethany. I made this purchase before a meal of the good Italian food with wine.

CHAPTER THIRTY-EIGHT

Back in Menton, the news from my contact was that our Prince had sailed. He would arrive in Monte Carlo in a few days. It was time for me to get to the poker tables to acquire information as to his habits.

The casino was not overly crowded in the poker room. I was able to get a seat in the private area segregated from the smaller limit games. Two of these areas had three tables each, while the third was one table, only for the very high-rollers. Two of the three tables where I was seated were in play.

I bought in the game for three thousand euros. This seemed about average for the other nine players. My play was very conservative. I wanted to have a lot of table time to discreetly get info on the Prince.

Sometimes the poker dealer, often a female, is more interested in talking than dealing. I was lucky. Serena, our dealer, was a talking machine. Once I got in a question about very high-stakes players, she proceeded to name several including Prince Abdul. I did not have to ask another question to get the most important information. He owned a Bentley Mulsanne automobile, the extended wheelbase model for a large back seat, that stayed in the hotel parking garage for use when he was in Monaco. Serena also said he sometimes spent nights in the hotel. Other times on his yacht.

My preliminary thought was that I would smuggle a rifle, in small pieces, to be assembled for a long-shot kill as the Prince was leaving the casino. I had then realized this plan had a major flaw. The entirety of Monaco was very small. When such a politically important person was murdered, all exit routes could be easily blocked. As a casino and poker room patron, I would be subjected to police questions. I could not take any such chance.

Back in Menton, I returned my rental car. The following day I rented the most expensive automobile in stock, a Porsche. I needed a vehicle that would be valet-parked by the casino staff near other expensive autos.

My gardener contact at Fontana Rosa would now be put to work. I needed a five-pound powerful explosive to be held in place with a strong magnet. The explosion trigger would be radio controlled from a distance that needed to be at least three miles. I also would require a photo and diagram of the underside of the particular Bentley that transported the Prince. When I asked if all of this was possible in two or three days, the answer was that there was nothing I needed that would be impossible. In fact, he brought all I had asked in less than two days.

I went back to the casino before the arrival of the Prince. There was one detail that could ruin my plan. I handed the young man at the entrance of the parking garage a ten euro note as I asked to be allowed to walk through to view the expensive autos. My real purpose was to determine if there were security cameras. Luck was in. There were cameras for entrance and exit, but none inside where the cars were parked.

I studied in detail the underside of the type Bentley owned by the Prince. I had to locate an area to place the explosive that could not be seen even if the driver was so cautious as to use a mirror to check under the car. There was one small virtually hidden area where I could attach the explosive by the magnet.

On the day the Prince was to arrive, I put the explosive in the Porsche trunk before driving to the casino. Once the Bentley arrived, it was valet parked in the garage with my Porsche. The Prince, with the driver and another as his security, went directly to the poker room.

I walked to the parking area. When no one else was around, I told the attendant I needed to go in to get more money from my car. The usual ten euro note in my hand assured this request would be granted. Inside, I got the explosive, quickly sliding under the Bentley to make the placement. From entrance to my exit of the garage took less than one minute.

I played poker for awhile. I knew our Prince would be at his table for hours. I would just hope this was a time he would stay at the dock.

After several hours, I left in my automobile to park at an overlook in France just outside the boundary of Monaco. The overlook gave a clear view of the road leading from the casino down to the harbor. There was sufficient road light to identify cars using my binoculars. I had to be careful not to fall asleep or lose focus.

About four o'clock in the morning I spotted the Bentley on the road. I just had to hope the Prince was in the auto and had not decided to stay in the hotel. I pressed the trigger mechanism. There was an almost instantaneous huge explosion lighting the sky above the roadway. I had either assassinated a Saudi Prince or only his driver.

I drove immediately to Menton. The news reports were coming. Saudi Prince Abdul had been killed in a motor vehicle explosion after leaving the casino in Monte Carlo. My body shivered as I heard the report. I had become a successful assassin for the CIA "Kill Squad".

Before I had been sent to Monaco, Contact Red had started fake internet chatter that a terrorist group in Iraq was going to attack Saudi's royalty for their association with the United States. In all the news reports for weeks to follow, there was no mention of possible U.S. involvement in the murder of the Prince. In fact, one terrorist group actually claimed responsibility.

My instructions were to leave Menton by the six to seven hour train ride to Paris. I was then to stay in Paris for one week during which I would act like

the normal tourist. Not bad duty before flying back
to New York.

CHAPTER THIRTY-NINE

Since I would arrive from France on a Sunday, I changed to a direct flight to Boston. I wanted to see Bethany without waiting for the following weekend. She had to break a Sunday date. I admit to worrying that absence may not make the heart grow fonder. Whatever, nothing had changed while I was gone. From arrival on Sunday until she had to leave for Monday work, we were totally in love.

She really liked the cashmere sweater from Italy. It would wear nicely on the cool Boston evenings. Since it was a gift from me, she joked it would be her "chastity" sweater. When she wore it on a date, the man would not be able to talk her into taking it off. Very funny!

She had some interesting information. Margo did not want the "work your ass off" life of an associate in the private law practice. She had taken a lawyer position with the legal department of the City of New York. Forty hours per week with a reasonable salary and benefits. But guess how she obtained the position? She was seeing Nucci. This was inconsistent with her previous statements about not getting into a long relationship with a married man.

It seems she needed a strong recommendation because of the number of applicants. She called Nucci for help. He did help with no strings attached. Margo actually suggested they could have an occasional liaison. She told Bethany she liked being escorted to expensive places like the casino with all its amenities in Connecticut. Once each month or so would be a good change from the beer and pizza dates.

Nucci was very honest with her. He would never divorce Rosa. He would not allow an affair with her to embarrass Rosa. Within those conditions, they could have some fun.

When I got back to the Bronx, it was not any too soon, as Mother was now in rapidly declining health. I was so glad to be there when she died in a couple-of-weeks. Now the family was me, my sister, her husband, and my soon to be born nephew or niece. I was really pleased for Anna that she was pregnant.

It was exactly two weeks after the funeral that I got my next call from Contact Red.

CHAPTER FORTY

Contact Red outlined a situation needing immediate attention. I would be taking a vacation trip with a tour group to Ecuador and the Galapagos Islands. My story would be that I had an inheritance from parents who were now both deceased. I was into extensive travel.

I would have been thrilled to have such a trip if it did not involve a travel purpose that was to murder someone.

One of the numerous political parties in Ecuador was the Democratic Left.
A high-level member of this organization was Alvaro Zambrano. He was traveling the country holding meetings and making speeches. It was obvious that he planned to be a candidate for President.

The big problem for the United States was not just that he was a socialist, a social democrat, but that he was very much in the pocket of the Russians. He was often seen entering and leaving the Russian Embassy. CIA intelligence had confirmed that his campaign expenses would be substantially funded by the Russian government.

Russia had long wanted a foothold in South America. Alvaro and Ecuador was a good opportunity. Alvaro was well-liked. With a lot of campaign money, he would be among the favorites.

The United States had an on and off relationship with the Ecuadorian government over the years. This was not a major problem until now. Russian control of a country in South America would cause substantial security problems which could not be allowed.

The tour group that Contact Red had booked for me would spend one day in Quito, Ecuador before flying to the Galapagos for a one-week exploration. This week coincided with the week Alvaro was scheduled to be in the Islands for a combination of politics and vacation.

I was given a lot of reading to do before leaving. I had to be knowledgeable to avoid any suspicion that I was not an ordinary tourist. There was much history here.

The Galapagos Islands are a part of Ecuador, though lying quite a distance off the coast, one thousand kilometers to the west. There are eighteen major islands, twenty-one in total, with five inhabited by about twenty-five to thirty thousands residents of Ecuador.

From the capital city of Quito, our group would fly to San Cristobal Airport on the islands before boarding our boat. We would sleep and eat on the boat and be tendered in to the islands each day.

From my reading, I had learned why my group would want such a long trip.

Charles Darwin made two trips to the Islands in 1835 before completing his famous book "On the Origin of Species." Development of his theory of evolution clashed with some religious beliefs that has carried over to be a matter of controversy and argument to present days. I had some memory of hearing in school classes of the "Scopes Monkey Trial" where a Tennessee high school teacher, John T. Scopes, was tried in 1925 for the crime of teaching evolution.

With much demand from the religious Christians

dominant in that state, the Tennessee legislature had passed into law the "Tennessee Butler Act" making unlawful any teaching of human evolution in the public schools. The Galapogas Islands had contributed to the factual findings that threatened the literal account of the creation found in the Christian Bible.

What Darwin found is still to be seen by today's occupants and visitors to the Islands. The Galapagos giant tortoise is the largest living species in the world. Some weigh over nine hundred pounds. Galapago means tortoise in Spanish. Though the same animal, their shell size and shape varies between the islands. On islands with humid highlands, the tortoises are larger, with domed shells and short necks. On islands with dry lowlands, the tortoises are smaller, with "saddleback" shells and long necks. Darwin saw that the same tortoise had evolved differently over thousands or millions of years. Some of the tortoises live for more than one hundred years. One is known to have survived for at least one hundred seventy years.

Darwin also found this type evidence of evolution with the so-called "Darwin finches". The same species of bird had developed different beaks to be able to best feed on the food sources of the island they occupied.

While the Galapagos are known for their importance to Darwin's theory, his research had continued for more than twenty years before his famous book was published in 1859. The tortoises and finches were only parts of the facts leading to the conclusion.

My assigned duty was to assassinate Alvaro Zambrano. In the matter of the Saudi Prince, the way to carry out the kill had been left to me. For the situation in Ecuador, the CIA had a definite plan in place. This was to be the third time Alvaro had set aside a week to spend in the Islands. He was noted to be a lover of snorkeling, spending every afternoon in the clear waters where the volcanic island rock rose from the sea. His history was that he would snorkel alone for several hours at a time.

I would take normal snorkeling equipment on the trip. After we cleared customs in Quito, an agent would furnish me with a small oxygen diving tank and an electroshock weapon. This weapon was the size and shape of a small pistol. It would be pressed against a person's body and fired. The shock would be incapacitating, disrupting the muscle function.

Each day I would go to the island Alvaro had on his schedule. When he went to a snorkeling site, I would follow, keeping a good distance. Once he was in waters that could not be observed from the land, I would swim to him, fire the electroshock, and drag him underwater. With my diving oxygen tank, I could stay under for fifteen to twenty minutes. When he was dead from drowning, I would swim underwater as far away as I could on the remaining oxygen. If all went well, I would be back on my boat before he was found.

This would be a time when all did go well. I accomplished my assassination precisely as planned. I was back on our boat for dinner when the news arrived that Alvaro had drowned while snorkeling. In the days following, there was not a question raised as to the death being anything but an unfortunate accident.

My group returned to Quito for the remainder of our tour. I left the electroshock weapon and the empty oxygen tank filled with water at the bottom of the Pacific ocean.

Safely back in Quito, I could enjoy the remainder of this tour. That is, until our plane would leave through the small gap in the high mountains around the Quito airport. Flying in was scary. Out would be worse.

In the mountains above the city, we went to a large rose-growing business. There we found acre after acre of many varieties of roses. The owners, a couple, lived in the beautiful home built by her parents. The story was that the building materials had been brought through the mountains by pack mules decades before.

The owners asked if we could guess the country that was the biggest source of their annual sales of about fifteen million stems. The United States was the most common guess. No one got the correct answer. The county of Russia bought more of their roses than any other.

The last of our trip was north into the country of Peru. There we found Machu Picchu, the ancient Incan city in the Andes mountains. This was quite a sight. We were fortunate to get there. Mud slides often block access to the location from Ecuador.

Ecuador is a long way from New York. Our tour did not have first or business class seating on the airplane. In addition, we had to land in Miami to clear U.S. customs. There was another stop in Atlanta for some of our group to disembark. I was pleased with the success of this venture, but I was ready for some time in the Bronx.

CHAPTER FORTY-ONE

Back in New York, my first order of business was to call Bethany. On my business trips, I was instructed not to take my cell phone. I was only to use the thirty day "burner" phone furnished to call Contact Red, if necessary, and nobody else.

Hearing Bethany's voice was the top of my day. She told me that my return from "whatever work I had, wherever it might have been" was perfectly timed. Margo had called about the next weekend. She was going back to the hotel/casino in Connecticut with Nucci for Friday and Saturday nights. We were invited. Bethany had worked very hard to have enough client billings for the week in order to leave work early on Friday. She would just smile while refusing to tell me what she was going to do if I had not returned in time to be her date.

I inquired as to what was going on with Margo and Nucci. Nothing had changed. They would get together once or twice per month. No obligations. Margo just liked a little life of the rich and famous. Nice hotel suites, expensive food, impressive wine, and such. This was just more appealing to her than the ordinary dates with young males expecting to spend little money for their hope to get laid. She said her arrangement with Nucci was somewhere past being a slut, probably closer to a prostitute, but she simply did not care.

Nucci and Margo came by for me in the limo on the way to get Bethany at her train stop from Boston. On the ride of two hours or so, the champagne flowed and the conversation was light. Later that night, Bethany told me, without asking, that something made her think that Nucci might have some knowledge of my work trips. Very perceptive of my smart and beautiful young lady.

We were rushed to get in our rooms and change for dinner. As expected, Nucci had us in the most elegant restaurant in the hotel. In a small separated area for a table of four, we had the head waiter for our entire meal. As was not unexpected, Nucci had planned dinner. Perhaps to impress Margo and, if so, his work was as intended.

Our waiter was well-versed to state each course in Italian before explaining in English. He commenced with aperitivo, a small prosecco to be enjoyed before food was served.

Next came the antipasto, in English "before the meal", at our table consisting of cheese, sopprasatta, and bread. This was a night to be very hungry.

The primo now arrived, pasta served as an appertizer, which for us was a choice of ravioli Florentine or truffle pasta. Except for Nucci, we all wanted to try the truffle pasta dish. We made a nice choice.

It was now time for the main course, the secondo. Nucci took over from the waiter to talk about this part of the meal. He had arranged a choice of veal chops or cernia which is grouper fillets coated with flour and cooked with lemon flavored oil and sage. Nucci and I asked for the veal as Bethany and Margo wanted the fish. Nucci then ordered a bottle of barolo, a heavy red wine, for the veal, and bardolino, a lighter red to accompany the fish. Our waiter nodded his agreement with the food and wine. He would select the contorno, a platter of vegetables which would pair well with both veal and fish.

This fabulous meal ended with the dolce, a choice of sweets, always served with coffee, followed with degestivo, at our table the liqueur limoncello.

It was now only a few minutes before the midnight show, a performance of the classic Cabaret. Acting like teenagers with a parent's credit card, Nucci and Margo were off to the showroom. Bethany and I begged off to head for our room.

The next morning was filled with beautiful sunshine. As usual, Nucci was headed to the poker room and Margo to the pool. Bethany and I had an early morning liaison in the bed (we had been too tired following last night's meal), a light breakfast, and were on our way to walk along the river.

Bethany was unhappy with one aspect she had learned of the practice of law.

She was working very hard, with long hours, as she met her obligation to bill clients for a minimum of seventy hours per week. She was consistently among those first to arrive at work in the mornings. She was staying in her office to nine or ten on week-nights, and was there on Saturday, along with many Sundays.

Not all, but many of the other associates, could be

seen leaving for the bars by or before six o'clock. It was not possible to keep such office hours and meet the client billing requirement. There was no question. They were billing clients for work that was not done.

The partners in the firm had to be aware of what was going on. They knew, but did not object. How many partners were also cheating clients with their hours billed for work that had not been done? She was just upset to learn that, in her chosen profession, making money was often more important than the clients being represented.

I disliked seeing her unhappy about anything. Other than expressing sympathy, it was difficult for a former loan shark to criticize money being more important than the client.

With the sun shining, birds chirping, and walking hand-in-hand with Bethany, I was very happy. Our conversation changed. Bethany was about to start a litigation where she would assist a partner who was in charge of the case. This trial would last at least a month, perhaps longer, in court all day and preparation at night for each following day. With weekend preparation, she would be occupied seven days a week. She hoped I would come to Boston for a few days until the day and night trial preparation commenced. I would definitely do that.

Now my smiling friend changed to another topic. Marriage. Was I still considering her marriage proposal?

What Bethany did not know, and what I could not disclose, was that I was partially through with the commitment I had made to the CIA. I had completed two of the five assassinations promised in my talks with Contact Red. I had no way of knowing the time involved before the next and thereafter. I could not be sure I would not be killed in one of the remaining assignments.

I could, and did, tell Bethany that I wanted her, and wanted to be her husband, more than anything. I was sworn to secrecy, even as to the time involved, but she would be proud of me when she could know about my "job." As soon as possible her marriage proposal would be accepted. She laughed as she reminded me her proposal had an out if she found a rich man in Boston who was good in bed.

The CIA was depositing a monthly salary amount

in my offshore bank account that was very generous. I was living good with money being saved. The money that would allow us to live our lives in financial comfort came from the completion of each assassination. There was a three-hundred thousand dollar additional deposit following each successful assignment. I would have enough money for us to buy a home and live without her having to continue working as a Boston lawyer.

We concluded the river walk to have lunch at the pool with Margo. Nucci was taking her to an early dinner so they could go to a dance featuring old rock and roll music. Nucci never ceased to surprise me.

With a couple of wines during the meal of blackened redfish, Bethany and I decided to take an afternoon nap.

We declined an offer to join Nucci and Margo. It was just too tempting to order room service, a good bottle of wine, and spend the evening cuddled together in bed watching old movies.

The next morning, Bethany was left at the station for her train to Boston. I went home to pack to join her there. It turned out that we had only three days before my next call from Contact Red.

CHAPTER FORTY-TWO

George Solovani was born in Paris, France, where his father was working on assignment for the company in which he was a joint owner. The family soon returned to San Francisco, California. The Silicon Valley company was valued well in excess of one hundred million dollars and in the next ten years far exceeded one billion. As an only child, George became a billionaire while still in college when his parents were killed in an automobile wreck.

George was the epitome of a spoiled child. He had a mother who allowed anything and a father too busy in business to pay attention. He had few friends in high school and was generally thought of as an obnoxious ass.

A large contribution to a new high school football stadium assured his failing grade record would be altered to meet college requirements. Even then, there was a substantial bribe to a University admissions official to record a test score sufficient to meet requirements for enrollment.

In college, George had no male friends. He used the unlimited money from his mother to garner dates with girls who would accept him because of his spending. Expensive meals, shows, concerts, or perhaps offers of a weekend trip to Hawaii were often accepted.

With his inheritance in hand, he left college for Hollywood. He had an idea of becoming a movie actor but lacked any of the work ethic for success. With all of his faults, George was smart. If he could not be an actor, he could be surrounded by actors, especially females. He bought controlling interest in a movie production company.

As far back as my high school days, there were jokes about the movie "casting couch" where aspiring young actresses spread their legs for a chance at movie stardom. George became very adapt at using his position and power for sexual favors.

In Hollywood, money and power is enough to have contact with the elite, the actors, directors and producers. George had learned to use his money well. He had also become among the movie industries most liberal, change- America proponents.

I was listening intently to Contact Red as he described George Solovani for close to an hour. I knew well enough that he was not wasting time in idle conversation, so the reason would be forthcoming.

Contact Red continued as he described George's change of interest from aspiring women to young girls. Parents of teenage girls dreamed of their child's movie stardom. George offered to audition the young star hopefuls, but only in private without parents or other adults present. His stated contention was that he needed to determine their maturity in addition to talent. When he prevailed sexually, the young girl was warned never to speak of the relation. He would deny and any attempt to implicate him would result in a permanent ban from the movie industry.

He made one very bad choice. When a most attractive fourteen-year-old girl resisted his advances, he raped her. Over his threats, she went to her parents who called police. The rape examination revealed the perpetrator had not used a condom. With the victim's testimony added to the DNA evidence, George could be looking at a long time in prison.

A friend in the prosecutor's office called George with a warning that arrest would happen in a day or two. The warning was in time. Using his private jet, he was in Paris before the arrest warrant could be served. He was a joint citizen of both the United States and France. France would not extradite any French citizen regardless of the charges.

While the description of George was that of a piece of human shit, I still did not see a reason the CIA would be instructed to have him killed. Contact Red then disclosed what was going on. George Solovani was a communist, but not just any communist. His money was the substantial funding source of several communist organizations in the United States. Since he could not return to the United States without being prosecuted, his hatred of America had boiled over. He wanted a revolution to overthrow the government. Not a social revolution, a violent warfare revolution to take over the United States by force.

The CIA had intercepted messages whereby he cited the February 1917 revolution in Russia when the Bolsheviks murdered and displaced the rulers of that country. He wanted the same for America. Revolt and kill all of the national leadership. Take over and install a communist government. He could then return to a position of leadership.

He would fund other radical groups to promote riots for any or no reason to instill fear throughout the population. Divide the people, then conquer by force.

The President had decided that George was a substantial terrorist threat to the United States. National security required this threat to be eliminated. I was to be the eliminator by way of assassination.

George had settled in Paris. He purchased a large estate outside Paris with his home fully surrounded by a stone fence with gated entrance. There was electronic security everywhere. Add in guard dogs with several on premises guards. George knew the United States had killed a number of terrorists abroad. He was leaving nothing to chance.

I flew to France in the guise of a tourist. I had an advantage of not being known as a member of the CIA Kill Squad. I took a month occupancy of an Airbnb apartment in the city. I would first look for any routine followed by George in his new environment.

There was a local bar near the estate where George now resided. I had learned over my years that people who frequent bars as their social outings like to talk. Fortunately for me, a lot of French people speak English as a second language. It only took a second visit for the bar patrons to warm to me. Conversation flowed.

George and his rich lifestyle was a common discussion. I learned that he liked expensive restaurants, the opera, and French women, one in particular. Claudette Laurent was a beautiful twenty-three-year-old former drama student who was having some local success in small productions. The word was that she thought George could be her entry into Hollywood or Broadway acting roles.

I learned she lived in a nice, but old-style, apartment building located just out of the expensive districts. George was reputed to spend one or two nights each week at her living quarters. He often took Claudette to dinner at Au Petit Cadoret, a very fine and expensive restaurant, followed by an opera performed at the French National Opera House in Paris.

There are two primary considerations for an assassin. The obvious is to plan and carry out the kill. The second is to be able to escape or disappear without being discovered. I did not intend to spend the remainder of my days in a French prison.

With information obtained over beer and wine at the bar, together with my observations of the estate, it became apparent that success at George's home was unlikely. He traveled in a heavily armored limousine that was kept in a garage attached to the house. He could leave and return in the limo without any outside exposure.

I moved to exploring the possibility of taking him out at the opera. The opera house was huge with a seating capacity of more than two thousand. I bought a seat on the main floor to attend an opera named Rigoletto. I wanted be there in a crowd to observe seating and movement within the building during a performance. It did not take long to realize that this would not work. There were numerous private boxes on each side extending a number of levels above the main floor. George would certainly have a box. I would not be able to locate him if I could gain access to the floors above. Even if I could, getting out would be impossible.

I did learn that opera was not for me. Rigoletto was in three acts by someone named Giuseppe Verdi. The primary characters were a Duke, the hunchback court jester Rigoletto, and his beautiful daughter Gilda. The singing was in Italian with a screen above the stage showing the words in French. I did not understand the story and left after act one. It could have been interesting to stay for the last song at the end. In New York Yankee baseball I had often heard the phrase "the opera ain't over till the fat lady sings."

CHAPTER FORTY-THREE

Having ruled out George's estate and the opera house as beings sites for my assignment, I found the location of the apartment building where Claudette Laurent lived. It was as described, a five-story older brick building with wooden interior stairs, without an elevator. I particularly noted that there was an absence of security cameras. There was nothing that Americans would call modern, no guard or door attendant, older door locks, no fire alarms, and actually no fire escapes.

On my previous trip to Paris, I had asked about the lack of fire escapes. The best answer I received was that Paris rarely had fires. My thought was that unlucky residents on upper floors would have a choice of death by fire or by jumping out a window.

Claudette's apartment was on the third floor. I could easily pick any lock in the building. Each floor had a storage room where I could hide at night until George and Claudette came in from their evening and were in bed asleep. The information I had was that the limo would bring them to her building. The driver and a guard would sleep in the parked automobile until George was ready to leave the following morning.

I now had the best place. I would watch the estate for the limo to leave. Assuming the route was to Claudette's residence, I would hide in the third-floor storage closet awaiting their return.

It was three nights later that the limo left on the expected route to get Claudctte. I was in the closet for more than five hours when I heard the arrival of a loud and highly intoxicated couple. I stayed in the closet until three o'clock that morning before entering the apartment. The couple was naked on her bed in a sound sleep.

The body of George only jerked slightly as my knife cut deeply through his artery and vocal cord. My assassination was complete. I was pleased Claudette did not move as I did not want to have to kill her. It would be bad enough for her to wake in the morning with a horrible hangover and a naked dead man covered with blood in her bed.

I eased out of the building without encountering anyone. The two men in the limo appeared to be asleep. I was back in my rental unit before the sunrise.

By noon, the television news in Paris was all about the murder of George Solovani. Claudette was too upset to be interviewed. The tabloids were printing special editions speculating that the murder was by a jealous boyfriend of hers. Every male she had been known to date was named as a suspect.

Television and newspaper reporting had some speculation that the United States could have involvement, but I was secure in that there was no proof available in an investigation. I would stay the remainder of my Paris rental to avoid being identified among those leaving France shortly after the time of the murder.

It was very good news when the reports were that George had not left a will. With no wife or siblings involved, his cousins, and the French government, would be in legal fights over his money for years to come. His groups of communists in the United States would have no claim to the fortune.

CHAPTER FORTY-FOUR

Arriving back in the Bronx, I learned that Bethany was about one week from the conclusion of the trial that had dominated her life for weeks. She simply would have no time for me until then. But, she was to be allowed two weeks vacation at the trial conclusion and wanted to spend most of it with me following a couple of days for a family visit.

I could stay with her in Boston, she could stay with me in New York, or we could take a trip somewhere, anywhere. My choice.

There was no way I was not taking her offer. The only question was what we would do. I did not know when or for how long my next assignment would be. After a lot of thought, it was time for me to plan something special for her. I now had money. I would come up with a trip we would always remember.

It was the winter cold in New York which I had known all of my life. Her home in Iowa can be cold also, but she now had years of experience in New

York and Boston weather.

I was researching travel on the internet. We did not have time for travel to other continents, so I was mostly looking at the warmer United States in the south. Somehow I came across Canada, Quebec City and Montreal. This would be very cold, more so than New York and Boston, but a new experience for both of us. Decision made. I considered including her in the planning, but she was covered up in the trial.

Anyway, my decision was to plan every detail that I thought would make our trip fun and outstanding while enjoying each other being together. I called to tell her to pack her warmest winter clothing with hats, gloves, jackets, pants, long underwear, and bring her passport. In typical fashion, her one question was whether she could take off the long underwear when we were in bed together.

Her trial was finally over, her family visit complete, and we arrived in Quebec City, Canada.

She questioned my sanity as I told her our first night would in a hotel room made entirely of ice.

Located outside of the city is the world renown Quebec Ice Hotel, Hotel de Glace. Made entirely of snow and ice, the hotel is rebuilt each year. The melting structure takes about five days to destroy and some fifty-five days to build again the following winter.

We checked in at the nearby Hotel Valcartier which furnishes a regular heated room with each rented room in the Ice Hotel. Tourists have a lot of luggage which does not fare well in the ice quarters freezing rooms. Electronics are very vulnerable to such cold. After storing luggage, we were taken to our ice room.

The ice bedrooms have no doors, but a pull curtain provides privacy. We were told that noise is not a problem as most quests retire quietly into the hollow silence one would expect of an igloo.

Bethany looked at the beds, two singles, made of solid ice with a wooded boxspring and mattress set on top. She could not stop laughing. However, I did detect a lot of happiness in that laughter. I was confident I had done well with this unusual choice for the first night in Canada.

The instructions from the Ice Hotel staff were to snuggle into a furnished sleeping bag without undressing. The bag plus clothing should keep you warm through the night. There was a suggestion not to drink too much as need for toilet relief after going to bed could be a problem. The room had no facility. Flush toilets, together with electricity, male/female changing rooms, hairdryers, and lockers were in a heated structure adjacent to the outdoor hot tubs and sauna.

Considering the toilet problem, we decided to do our drinking early in the evening. The Ice Bar was very popular. Everything in this bar was made of ice except for the beverages. All drinks were served in glasses made entirely of ice. Gloves were necessary in order to hold a cocktail.

Tours of the facility stop in the early evening. At that point the music starts and the hotel is turned over to those brave enough to stay the night.

A vodka martini seemed a good choice to start our evening. Bethany was clearly happy that I had planned the trip. She asked me not to tell what other days would bring. She wanted each to be a surprise. Having noticed the ice wedding chapel, she told me that she would need to shop for something "virgin white" if I was planning a really big surprise.

A second martini followed as we held hands, listened to music, and simply relaxed into the evening.

The hotel Valcartier had a nice restaurant where we enjoyed Atlantic salmon accompanied by pinot noir, dessert and an after dinner brandy.

Then we were on to the Valcartier room to get bathing suits and toiletries to take to the heated structure. There was the hot tube under the stars before the true experience of trying to sleep in a room made of ice.

From the hot tub, one could see that the Ice Hotel is a unique, fairytale type of structure. The work and artistry in the erection was truly impressive, and the interior lighting gave a glorious glow through the thick ice and snow.

After relaxing in the hot tub, we went back into the heated building to dry off before putting on our full clothing to go to bed. If we were to wake up in the night, there was an option to go back to the

Valcartier for a normal bedroom. Bethany and I were both stubborn enough to stay the entire night no matter how difficult.

At six in the morning, we both were awake and making fast time to the outside toilets before moving to our heated room.

With this great experience complete, we were on to the next day of our plan.

CHAPTER FORTY-FIVE

I had three activities planned for this day. After our early departure from the Ice Hotel, we moved to the warm hotel room where we undressed. Deciding that an undressed state was a good opportunity for sex that was not possible in the ice beds, we took that opportunity before showers, dressing, and breakfast at the hotel.

We moved to a somewhat small room in a quaint hotel in the center of town. After getting our luggage stored, we walked to the Citadelle of Quebec, also known as La Citadelle. This defensive fortification was originally built by the French in the seventh century. It sits atop Cap Diamant overlooking the river.

I was very interested from a military standpoint. Bethany listened intently as I told her the information I had accumulated before our guided tour began. I did not believe she was sincerely interested in the military history. I was pleased that she was willing to brave the cold to be with me.

Our tour guide was a pleasant older man who was entertaining and most knowledgeable. He asked our group about language, French or English. We were in luck that all understood English as a first or second language. The dominant language in Quebec City was French as it would be in Montreal, our next location.

We learned that the Citadel has the oldest military building in Canada. It forms part of the fortifications that still surround Quebec City. This city and Campeche in Mexico are the only cities in North America still having such surrounding fortifications.

Following the French, there was British control of the fort and Quebec City after their conquest of New France. They constructed the modern Citadel for defense against a potential American attack. In 1871, the British gave the property to the Canadian government.

By the time our tour was over, we were very cold. We thawed in our hotel room before having lunch and a short nap. Bethany was all smiles as I explained that the remainder of our time in the city would be indoors except for short walks to the destinations.

The afternoon took us to the Cathedral-Basilica of Notre-Dame de Quebec, the oldest church in Canada. I was not the best Catholic around, but I did have some historical interest in the church which I attended with my parents and sister.

There is a crypt in the church in which some governors and the bishops of Quebec are buried.

I thought the most interesting history was that the church was destroyed twice by fire, once in wartime during the 1759 Siege of Quebec, and a second time in 1922 by the Canadian faction of the Ku Klux Klan. I had no idea that the KKK extended into Canada.

The inside of the church was everything a visitor would expect. This was a christian story told in the form of art. I could see that Bethany was enjoying this choice more than the fortress.

After about an hour, we ventured back into the cold, walking to our hotel to prepare for dinner. I had selected a restaurant that could have been the best in Quebec City. If not the absolute best, it had no competition as the most expensive.

Bethany had brought a couple of nice dresses for evening wear, but this was not the climate to wear anything except blouse, sweater, and a second sweater, with pants over long underwear. Her great figure was not obvious under so many clothes, but she still looked exceptional. My dress was similar to hers, and we both had overcoats and hats.

From my research in several sources, Restaurant Taniere was ranked in the top tier of all in Quebec City. We were seated at a table for two with a window view of the sidewalk and street.

In from the cold, we ordered before-dinner cocktails of Dewar's twelve- year-old blended Scotch whiskey over ice. Bethany added a twist of lemon to hers. The whiskey went well with the warmth of a fireplace. We were soon quite comfortable in our surroundings.

The drink was enjoyed while we studied the menu. Also the wine list. Our waiter had commenced in French but soon changed to English as he realized we were American tourists. We asked for a little time to make a decision.

I left the table for a visit to the men's room. Upon

return, Bethany handed me my menu. Since hers had no prices, she wanted to know what this evening would cost. She said I must have been really serious when I had told her I was making very good money in my secret employment. I just smiled and called her "nosy".

We both decided on tossed salad followed by a medium rare filet with garlic mashed potatoes. I ordered a 2015 pinot noir made by Foxtrot Vineyards in Okanagan, Canada. Neither of us had previously tried a Canadian wine. In fact, I did not know wine was produced in Canada. We were quite pleased.

We decided to skip dessert, but wanted the warmth of an after-dinner drink to fight off the cold of the walk back to the hotel. The decision was a glass of Grand Marnier, a cognac and orange liqueur.

Back at the hotel, the bar with its roaring fireplace was still open. We could not resist a night cap in front of the fire. At this time, I disclosed where we were headed in the morning. Montreal, Canada.

When we reached our bedroom, Bethany said I

had spent too much money taking her out for dinner. She laughed that men spending much less still expected sex, and so she hoped that I expected to have a lot of sex. I was well-provided.

CHAPTER FORTY-SIX

We arrived in Montreal in mid-afternoon. During the travel time, I gave Bethany a run-down on the factual information I had gathered about this major city.

Montreal is the largest city by population in Quebec. It is second to Toronto as the largest in Canada. It is the second-largest primarily French-speaking city in the world, after only Paris, France. French is the official language of the city.

Not being versed in the French language, I was pleased to read that Montreal is one of the most bilingual cities in all of Canada. In the entire Metropolitan area, about two-thirds of the people speak French at home compared to only about fifteen per cent speaking English. However, almost sixty per cent speak both French and English as necessary or convenient in public.

The city was founded in the seventeenth century as Ville-Marie or "City of Mary". The city is centered on the Island of Montreal, named after

Mount Royal, the triple-peaked hill in the heart of the city. Like a lot of settlements of that time, defensive position was important. Montreal had the defensive value of being an island with the high ground of the hill.

Montreal has several nicknames, among those being "City of Festivals", "City of Saints", "City of a Hundred Steeples", and "Sin City". I was curious about the latter. It's motto "Concordia Salus" translates to "well-being through harmony".

The taxi driver taking us to our hotel spoke English as well, maybe better, than I did. Our accommodations were somewhat larger than Quebec City and equally nice. We would settle in, bathe and dress for the evening.

Many people do not realize that some of the New York Broadway shows and musicals move on to Montreal. I had acquired two tickets about a dozen rows from the stage. We would have dinner in a small restaurant close to the theater district (not nearly as expensive as Quebec City) before attending "Fiddler on the Roof". I hoped Bethany had not seen this (she had not), but it is a classic that can be enjoyed more than once.

We followed the show with a drink in our hotel bar. After a discussion of "Fiddler", Bethany said she wanted me to know that she had never had sex in Montreal. I could take a hint, and we moved promptly to our room with its king-size bed.

CHAPTER FORTY-SEVEN

The following morning we arose for our day in Old Montreal (Vieux Montreal) which would commence with a horse carriage tour of several hours. We were dressed for the cold weather, but were pleased when our driver and guide furnished blankets for the ride. We were also pleased when he spoke excellent English.

Before we commenced moving to the various sites, he gave a background for Old Montreal.

The area has two blocks with cobblestone streets. The most famed of the buildings is the Notre-Dame Basilica, a grand Gothic Revival church built in the early nineteenth century, with a huge pipe organ and stained glass depicting scenes from the city's religious history.

Next to the Basilica is the Old Sulpician Seminary, constructed in 1685, which is Montreal's oldest building.

We commenced moving as our guide continued to

describe and give history.

To the east is Vieux-Port (the Old Port) which was once the main commercial harbor. It has now become a busy waterfront recreational area including a beach.

When we moved toward the north, we found Place Jacques-Cartier, a marketplace of decades before, which is now a very busy tourist area. It is lined with outdoor cafes and in warmer weather is filled with street performers, together with artists, artisans, portrait painters, and musicians. There were a few braving the cold to perform.

Near Place Jacques-Cartier is Champ-de-Mars Park, which is the site of the longest remaining section of the city's early fortification wall. Also nearby is Chateau Ramezay, the oldest private history museum in Quebec. The museum is in an early eighteenth century home of a former governor of New France. It has a beautiful French colonial style-garden as a feature of the property.

When we turned to the south, our guide described the Centre d'Histoire de Montreal. This museum has three floors of exhibitions designed to tell the city's story and is set within the renovated central fire station.

With all of its history, Old Montreal had become a hot spot for art and shopping. As to art, there was the DHC/ART gallery and the Centre Phi exhibition and performance venue. The names of the clothing boutiques were not known to me, Denis Gagnon, Reborn, Cahier d'Exercices, and Michel Brisson. Bethany knew of all and told me that I might be interested in Michael Brisson with its stylish suits and streetwear for men and in the men's labels at Reborn. I had no interest, but I could tell there would be a likely return for her to shop.

Completing our carriage tour, we went inside one of the cafes for a light lunch before the afternoon plan to visit Saint Joseph's Oratory

Oratoire Saint-Joseph du Mont-Royal is a Roman Catholic minor basilica. The basilica is a National Historic Site of Canada. It is the largest church in Canada with one of the largest church domes in the world. Tourist attraction is more than two million each year.

The Oratory is the tallest building in Montreal. It

rises more than thirty meters above the summit of Mount Royal. It had a special dispensation to violate the city building code which restricts most buildings to be only equal or less than the height of Mount Royal. The view we had from the Oratory was outstanding.

Our evening was to commence early at about five o'clock. There was a large bar near our hotel. We had noticed the after-work drinking crowd commenced their cocktails about that time and many continued for some two hours. We found two seats together at the bar.

At first we just enjoyed our drinks while listening to loud conversations primarily in French. After we had ordered second drinks, a woman from a nearby table asked if we were visitors to Montreal. When our response was affirmative, we were asked and accepted an invitation to join two couples. All four spoke English in addition to French.

The woman who asked us to join was a lawyer in the city. She and Bethany had much in common and the conversation flowed. When asked, I responded that I was employed by a government agency. Fortunately, the conversation moved on to the sites we had visited and then, as usual with men, to sports. Our new friends did not leave until eight. All six of us were well-lubricated with alcohol by the time we said goodbye.

In our condition, we decided room service at our hotel would be a comfortable conclusion to a fine day.

CHAPTER FORTY-EIGHT

Our next day could be fun or a complete disaster. At Mount Royal Park on the frozen Beaver Lake was ice skating. I knew that Bethany and I had both roller skated as children. Neither of us had put on a pair of ice skates. It just seemed to me that something so popular in Montreal should be tried.

I had arranged for a skating instructor to meet us at the stop for the 11 Bus to the lake at the park. My request for a female had been followed. We were met by a pleasant young girl about college age. Her English was a little broken, but adequate for communication.

At the lake, the first order of business was fitting skates to our shoe sizes. With skates in place, I tried to stand without success. With some instruction, we both were able to remain vertical for a short time. Moving required many falls. Eventually I was able to slowly skate around the perimeter of the skating area. Our instructor stayed with Bethany as she needed help to keep from falling. She was probably smarter than me, more personable, and clearly better-looking, but when it came to athletic ability, I was a long way ahead.

Bethany was only able to skate any distance without falling if the instructor stayed at her side. After she had suffered for about an hour, I called her torment to an end.

We had to wait about ten minutes for the 11 Bus to arrive for the short ride back to Old Montreal. I had anticipated that my girl would not remember this among our best moments together. But I had a survival plan. The Bota Bota in the Old Port.

Spa-sur-l'eau is a unique spa experience. On a boat anchored at the Quays of the Old Port of Montreal, Bota Bota offers the healing benefits of a spa on the beautiful St. Lawrence River. The spa is located on the five decks of a former ferryboat that had been converted to a show boat before the spa transformation.

The various spa installations include saunas with incredible views, steam rooms, outdoor whirlpool baths, cold showers and baths, with a gourmet snack counter, together with wine and other alcoholic drinks.

Available is massage therapy, body treatments, facial treatments, manicures and pedicures, as well as yoga and meditation.

We would take advantage of the personal attention items, massage, body and facial treatments. This was followed by a long sauna with a good amount of wine.

The usual smile had returned to Bethany's face. I knew I had recovered from the failed attempt to enjoy ice skating.

Back at the hotel, we both confessed to being too tired for a night out. It would be more wine, food by room service, and falling to sleep while watching a television movie spoken in French.

CHAPTER FORTY-NINE

The next morning, Bethany was not amused by my feeble attempt to convince her to dress for a morning trip to Les Laurentides, the snow ski Mecca for Montreal. Trying to learn to ski in one morning would not be in our plan for the day.

The Olympic Stadium had been constructed for Montreal to host the 1976 Summer Olympics. Attached to the Olympic Stadium is the Montreal Tower. This tower is five hundred forty-one feet high with a tilt of forty-five degrees. This makes the Montreal Tower the tallest inclined tower in the world. By way of comparison, the Leaning Tower of Pisa is a mere two hundred thirteen feet high with only a five degree tilt.

I could answer Bethany's question of how such a structure could stand. I had researched to find that the tower weighed almost nine thousands tons, but was anchored by almost one hundred sixty thousand tons of mass attached to its base as deep as thirty-three feet below ground.

We reached the tower top by a glass funicular to find a wonderful view of the Montreal skyline.

Leaving the tower, we moved to the Montreal Biodome. When the Olympics concluded, the purpose for much of the Park was transformed. The Olympic Velodrome became an indoor zoo, aquarium, and botanical gardens. The Biodome recreates five ecosystems, from the Amazon rain forest to the South Pole, all with temperature control, plants indigenous to the region, with its native wildlife.

Seeing all of the conversion of the Olympic Stadium was a full-day activity which we both enjoyed.

That night we would try another venture into the Montreal theater district. In my trip research, I had found a concert at the Corona Theatre by the Beach Boys. I was surprised as my first thought was that this group could not still be performing after so many years. The answer was that only one or two of the original group was performing, but the songs would be the classics from years before.

We found a small restaurant not far from the

Corona for a before-concert dinner. The house specialty was broiled or baked fish of several varieties from the cold Atlantic waters. Adding a choice of sauce made for a very tasty meal when accompanied by a white wine recommended by our waiter. After sharing a chocolate dessert, we were ready for music from the rock and roll era.

I think there was only one original member of the Beach Boys, but this was not an issue. The music was great. Bethany and I knew many of the old songs that were classics.

We left the Corona in a fine mood with energy left for a drink at our hotel bar. We had one more day and night in Canada before returning to New York.

As we had enhanced our evening by staying awake for some male/female bedroom activity, we slept into mid-morning. After a light breakfast, followed by dressing in warm clothing, we set out for a day exploring the business and residential districts of the city. We would walk to take in as much of the local flavor as possible.

I may have previously mentioned that the broader

metropolitan area of Montreal exceeds four million. The city, including all the other municipalities on the Island of Montreal, is about two million population.

Although Toronto has surpassed Montreal in commercial activity and population, Montreal remains a major center of commerce. The city, Ville de Montreal in French, is heavy in finance, pharmaceuticals, technology, aerospace, design, education, art and culture. I was interested that gaming was also available in several casinos.

We spent the remainder of the morning through a late lunch in the business district before moving to some of the residential areas. We were walking in highly populated neighborhoods near the business district, so we had little to make comparisons to New York or Boston. I did feel the pace of life might be somewhat slower.

For our last night of entertainment, I had gambled on musical artists known as "Home Free Vocal Band". The Majestic Theatre had this a cappella group featuring country music. This could be good or bad. My gamble worked. We stayed until completion with much applause from the audience of the sold out performance.

CHAPTER FIFTY

The next morning commenced our return to the United States. Bethany had a couple of days left before starting back at work in Boston. She would stay these days with me in the Bronx.

During our return, conversation was mostly about our adventures in Canada and the super fun we had. Without needing to verbalize, we both knew our relationship had evolved into magical mutual love, probably long before Canada, but now without any doubt. We would have long talks the next two days with nothing but dinner plans for the two evenings.

The first evening was dinner with Nucci and Rosa. He had found a recently opened restaurant with a New Orleans flair. There was a normal New Orleans/Cajun menu, but with an option only found in a couple of restaurants in the southern city. The option was "feed me". With this order, the waiter would bring a number of dishes one at a time. Each was a delicious surprise. I did not keep count, but there were at least seven or eight. This was a real treat and, as usual, Nucci insisted on paying the check.

The conversation was mostly about our time in Canada. However, Rosa was not one to lose an opportunity to push for the permanent relationship she was convinced that Bethany and I should have. We mostly avoided answers, but did confess we were talking about our future.

During these two days before Bethany had to return for work in Boston, we agreed it was truly love for each other that should move into marriage. I could not disclose the details of my work. I was quite sure I never wanted to tell her I was being paid to assassinate perceived enemies of the United States. The Division within the CIA that I was working for was also top secret.

I could and did tell her I had committed to five work contracts. I had completed three with two remaining. When these two were complete, I was promised a letter from a high federal government official thanking me for service, but more important, it would also state that all work activity by me following my army discharge was on specific order of the United States government. This would cover any questions about my being in the loan shark business. If any of the Boston high society had questions about my background, the answer would be that I did very secret work for our government. I really wanted this for Bethany.

Bethany did not want to wait for us to get married, but I prevailed in convincing her the wait would not be long. In fact, before we left for Canada, I was told my next assignment would be soon after the return.

Dinner the last night was with Margo. It was a pleasant red wine and spaghetti evening with a lot of conversation to catch up on our mutual lives. Margo was basically happy in her present position. Her job was adequate. Socially, she had more date invitations than she wanted. It was the typical young singles scene. The unattached males wanted to furnish an evening outing with an expectation of sex to follow. The married men just wanted to have a secretive sexual relationship.

She was still seeing Nucci once or twice each month. She really enjoyed this occasional affair. At least it was honest, none of the usual male bullshit involved. She laughed when saying she had wondered if she had inherited some "whore genes" through her family tree.

The next morning, I took Bethany to the train to Boston. We hated to part. I was ready to get through with my final two assignments.

CHAPTER FIFTY-ONE

It was only a few days after Bethany returned to Boston when I was notified of my meeting with Contact Red.

It is of interest that Bethany would have news of two occurrences that happened while I was on this next assignment. However, I would be getting ahead in my story, so this news will need to wait.

Contact Red commenced talking. I knew from our past that I was to listen until he opened discussion.

He asked if I was aware of the number of spies for the Chinese government that are in the United States. He answered his own question. Hundreds of thousands, perhaps one million or more. Some are traditional agents, trained in China and sent to our country with specific espionage assignments. The larger number are a result of the lax immigration laws long prevalent in the United States.

Several million Chinese have legally immigrated

to our country. Some have acquired U.S. citizenship or are working toward that end. Others have extended work permits or visas. A large number are technically educated with employment in fields where protected, classified or secret information is obtained in the course of job duties.

Contact Red explained that a majority of these came here with no intention of being involved in Chinese spy operations. But many, maybe most, left relatives in their homeland of China. They are asked to obtain secret, classified or protected information for the Chinese government. The leverage is their relatives. Threats of the Communist Party governing China are very serious. For example, a Chinese job holder in a classified position may be told his/her grandparents still living in China will be harmed if information is not obtained to be delivered to the Chinese government. These treats are not idle.

Such treats compel thousands to become unwilling spies, giving up information obtained in the course of employment.

With this general information out of the way, Contact Red moved on to more information leading to the assignment at hand.

He stated that one of the weak spots in our countries information security is in our liberal, which includes most all of the so-called elite, universities. Many Chinese college students come to the United States for their higher- level education. Many are very smart, coupled with excellent work ethics. Due to high academic success, they often are given student positions to work on government and industry research projects, many major, very important, which are supposed to be classified or even secret.

America's world class university system, according to some high-ranking intelligence officials, has become a soft target in the global espionage war with China.

A top counterintelligence official in our government has said that a lot of our ideas, technology, innovation and research is incubated on university campuses. Probably the majority of these universities getting research grants are very liberal within their faculties and administrations.

Our intelligence community is well-aware that Chinese students often are essentially spies sending research information to the Chinese Communist

Party. A high-ranking FBI agent has publicly stated that the Chinese purpose is to surpass the United States as the world superpower, and they are breaking numerous laws to get there.

Following the arrest of a dozen or more Chinese students for illegally sending results of grant projects to the Chinese, the FBI and other agencies have been pushing universities and research institutions to tighten policies governing confidentiality of research results. They are being asked to monitor outside relationships, travel disclosure and conflicts of interest for student researchers, graduate researchers, and professors.

This push, directed primarily toward the liberal universities, has been met by accusations of racial profiling and an overreaction to risks that make the American university system special. A nationally known university president may have spoken for the liberals when he publicly said he would not spy on his foreign-born students.

Now, the background was over, and he moved to the specifics of my next assignment. I was told that, of hundreds of Chinese spies the United States would like to eliminate, there was one at the top of the list. My assassination target would be a female.

Mingmei (meaning bright and beautiful girl) Wang was born in the U.S. of Chinese immigrant parents. When both parents were killed in an automobile accident, she moved to Beijing to live with her grandparents. She was age fourteen.

CHAPTER FIFTY-TWO

After high school graduation in China, Mingmei moved back to the United States to attend college at the University of California. She had an easy route to acceptance as her college entrance examination scores were at the top of the highest in the nation. In mental ability she was classified in the genius category. A full academic scholarship was accepted.

She enrolled with a major in microbiology. Her minor in computer science was unusual when coupled with the major, but she had the brain- power to handle any combination of studies.

Microbiology is the study of microscopic organisms, such as bacteria, viruses, fungi and protozoa. This includes fundamental research on the various aspects of microorganisms. Generally, this would be studies of bacteria, fungi, protozoa, algae, parasites, the immune system and viruses.

At this point, Contact Red apologized for the detail of Mingmei's study, but explained some knowledge would be important to understanding why she is presumed to be such a crucial target and other details of this different assignment.

He went on to tell me that she graduated with Highest Honors in her major field of microbiology. She also had perfect grade scores in the minor of computer science. With a University degree in hand, she moved on to graduate school seeking a masters degree concentrating in two specific areas of microbiology. These were virology: the study of viruses and immunology: the study of the immune system.

She would continue her educational pursuits into medical school. After completion of a medical degree in the shortest time allowed, Mingmei went on to become a nationally-known expert in the study of viruses and the human immune system.

Like many of the Asians studying in the United States, Mingmei had not a trace of social life. Her concentration on her studies was intense and all-consuming.

Her career move was to accept a teaching position as a full professor at Harvard University. She lived alone in a private townhouse development within walking distance of her office. Her class preparation and teaching was usual except she offered more detail than some of her peers.

It was her travel that first brought her to the attention of the counter-espionage units of our government. Billions of dollars in federal funds are handed out to universities and colleges for research projects vital to many areas of the U.S. economy and security. One such area is microbiology and the impact of viruses on the human immune system.

A lion's share of the research projects go to the universities considered among the most elite. As previously said, the elite are often the most liberal in social and political thinking, and teaching relevant subjects.

These research projects are generally assigned to faculty members who, in turn, use the most outstanding students and graduate assistants to participate in the work. Many of these are Asians, with a large number being native to China.

Homeland Security noticed a disturbing pattern. Mingmei was flown over the country to these universities to share her expertise in the research. In this capacity, she would have total access to all of the information and test results that had been accumulated for each project. She seemed to take particular interest in the research into the transmission to humans of the most deadly viruses.

The completion of the disturbing pattern was an abnormal number of trips to Beijing, China following her participation in these type studies. On one such trip, she was accompanied by a professor who was a Chinese national working in our country. This professor later had his visa terminated and was sent home to China. It had been discovered he had lied to the U.S. authorities by his denial of links to the Chinese government. He was actually a lieutenant in the Chinese military.

Our spies and informants in mainline China reported that there seemed to be a connection between her trips to China and developments in their laboratory research projects.

Then, there was the question of why she spent a year studying computer science. Might there be some secretive information sent by coded computer communication included in electronic mail to her relatives?

When all of the information available was given to the President, he was so convinced of her being a very important spy for China that her assassination was ordered.

CHAPTER FIFTY-THREE

Contact Red had a very serious look as he continued. The three world military powers, the United States, Russia and China, all have enough missiles armed with nuclear warheads to destroy the world. Nuclear attack by any of the three is deemed highly unlikely. Satellites would confirm the source of any missile launch and retaliation would be immediate. There would be massive destruction beyond any that could be acceptable to these countries.

Over the centuries of human population, there have been virus pandemics that have taken a heavy told on human life. At least once a pandemic was estimated to have killed two-thirds of the world population. As an aside, a doctor friend has maintained for years that the microscopic bugs will eventually kill the human race.

The potential of such deadly consequences has led much of the civilized world to agree to a ban against germ warfare under International Law. The world now has the Biological Weapons Convention and the Chemical Weapons Convention which have been generally ratified. These agreements prohibit the development, production, and stockpiling of biological and toxin weapons. Whether all of the agreeing countries are following the prohibitions is a matter of conjecture.

Unlike the launch of a nuclear weapon, the source of a virus may be impossible to determine. China could be working toward a virus that could be used as a weapon. In the modern world, the borders of our country are open to international travel and also porous to illegal entry. If such a weaponized virus was secretly introduced in mass in the United States, the U.S. could become so weak that war would not be necessary for China to become the dominant country in the world, their known goal.

This is the fear that led our President to order a kill even without conclusive evidence that Mingmei was a spy.

Our discussion now brought us to the major issues that made my assignment very different from the others.

On this job, I would be in constant contact with

Contact Red. I would be furnished a special cell phone that would call Contact Red when a code number was entered. This phone would not otherwise function. Also, the phone would internally destruct if an incorrect number was entered on the keypad.

If, at any time during the kill preparation, I gained information that our target might not truly be a spy, I would cease activity until my information was given to the President for his consideration.

Finally, the murder of Mingmei had to appear to be an accidental death. The Chinese could not know that this was an assassination of their operative. With the magnitude of spying by both the Chinese and United States, both countries knew and tolerated those deemed to be below critical status. We could not afford to get in a war of assassinations with the Chinese.

I was to study Mingmei, learn her habits, and make a plan for her death to appear to be an accident. I would be furnished any type of identity, with verifiable background, that I might select for these purposes. Since she lived in a private community, I was able to secure employment with the lawn care company which serviced the common areas. The community was large enough that I would work there most every day.

Her employer, Harvard University, is located in Boston. I would be living there, but would not be able to even contact Bethany to let her know I was near. This seemed so strange.

For two weeks, I mowed lawns while observing her habits as best I could. She was precise. Each weekday morning she left her home at seven-thirty to walk to Harvard, weather being irrelevant. She returned, also walking, at six in the evening. The lights to her town home were turned off at nine.

The first Saturday of the weekend involved walking to her office at nine in the morning. I did not work on the weekends, so I was able to follow her. I did not want to get too close, so I stayed on the outskirts of the campus. She must have had lunch at the school cafeteria as she did not leave for her home until five in the evening, again walking. Her lights were again off at nine.

Sunday was different. At eight in the morning, an automobile driven by a woman arrived at her town home. Mingmei immediately came out her door wearing knee length shorts and boots. She had on a baseball style hat, a long sleeve shirt, and a small backpack. I was not prepared to follow, but I could get the automobile make, model and license number.

Contact Red advised the automobile was registered to another professor at Harvard, also a Chinese national, who taught in the language department. My best guess was that she was going hiking. I waited for her return which was about nine that evening. I would be better prepared to follow the next weekend.

CHAPTER FIFTY-FOUR

The next six days were exactly the same as the Monday through Saturday before. Sunday was also the same except I was prepared to follow when the friend came by for Mingmei. I had a very ordinary automobile to follow at a safe distance avoiding any potential for discovery.

The two women traveled the short distance to the numerous hiking trails of the Blue Hills Reservation. I watched as they headed off in an easterly direction on a trail that seemed to have little activity. With this information about regular hiking, I now had the beginning of a plan to carry out the assassination in a manner that would not lend itself to questions of government involvement.

Not only would Contact Red have to give me approval and assistance, he would have to go back to the President as my plan would involve collateral damage, that is, the woman companion of Mingmei would also be killed. I was told that, after some discussion and thought, the President agreed that the importance of taking out Mingmei was sufficient justification to kill a woman who was likely no more than merely a friend caught in an unfortunate relationship.

The next week, Mingmei traveled to California to lend her advice to an ongoing research project. So, I would have to wait for another day of hiking to come into play.

I had to continue my work at the residential complex while she was gone. There would be a need for me to maintain a normal work scheldule waiting for an opportunity. The worst part was not the wait, but the fact I was so close to Bethany and unable to even let her know I was near.

My approved plan was to follow the women to their next hiking point. I had studied and had a printout of all the trails in the Blue Hills. I would have an automobile that could not be traced and another agent to assist. Upon arrival, I would watch for the trail the women would select. We would take a different trail from which we could cross to their route to wait in a heavily wooded area. Contact Red had confirmed there were no security cameras for the parking lot.

It was three weeks later that the Sunday hiking was back on. Luckily, they went again to Blue Hills. My plan was in motion.

From our vantage point, we could see the trail was not in use except for our two targets. When they came by, we were able to grab both, pulling them into the woods, where their throats and vocal cords were cut. My assisting agent took everything of value, wallets, credit cards, car keys, and cell phones. I hid the bodies in the deep woods while the agent went back to the parking lot. He took their car which would be later found several hundred miles away. I crossed several trails to come out in the parking lot some distance from the trail the women had selected.

I left in the car that I had been furnished to get to Blue Hills. I abandoned it some distance from Mingmei's home, walked some of the way, and boarded a bus to the Harvard area.

Mingmei's friend was married. When she did not come home that evening, her husband called the police. Their bodies were found the next morning. The stolen car would soon be found with their wallets, money and credit cards missing, along with

263

the cell phones.

My plan had worked to perfection. All of the news reports were that Mingmei and friend were the victims of a horrendous crime.

I would stay several more weeks working so that my leaving would have no possibility of connection to the crime. I spent several sleepless nights digesting the fact that I had murdered a woman not involved in the need to protect our country. I wondered if our President who gave the order felt any remorse.

I would take the train back to New York so to be in the Bronx when I called Bethany. I could never explain why I had been in Boston or even that I had been there for that time.

CHAPTER FIFTY-FIVE

It made me very happy to hear Bethany's voice answering my call. I did not think it was my imagination that she sounded like a woman in love (with me).

She said she had so much to tell me. The first had to be that some work she had done while I was doing "whatever I do" resulted in a bonus award of a week off work at a time she could select.

I interrupted to tell her to say no more. I would make plane reservations, and meet her at the Boston airport, for a few days at an island in the Caribbean. She should pack for warm island weather, and I would explain on the flight south. As with our Canada trip, most women would have asked dozens of questions. Bethany just said to let her confirm being away with her senior partner, and she would be ready.

The island I had selected was Migerousy located about one hundred miles north of Aruba. It was large enough to have a population of some fifty thousand permanent residents and an additional twenty thousand tourist capacity. It had an airport capable of international traffic, a financial district, considerable shops and restaurants, theaters, nice hotels, and good residential housing.

Migerousy is an independent island nation. It originally was settled by the English, becoming part of the British Empire. As the Empire contracted, Britain ceded the entire island to the residents, primarily of English origin, who established an independent country.

There were some early disputes over property ownership, but the newly formed government did well to settle disputes and establish legal order. The year round tourist business provided a good base for prosperity, but the largest overall business is the government owned Central Bank, the Bank of Migerousy. With no oversight or regulations except those established by the island government, the Bank was a haven for foreign depositors who were seeking a safe place to hide money.

The original currency of the island was the British Pound, but the government officials were smart to change to the United States Dollar as the official island currency. With this, all deposits in other currency was converted to the dollar which was often more stable in value and purchasing power.

All banking business, and every account, was private to the owners of the funds. There was a strict policy that no information would be released irrespective of the requesting body and reasons for the request. Somewhat similar to Swiss Bank Accounts, but even more information restrictive.

As we waited in the Boston airport for our flight, I had to explain why this sudden and particular trip.

I started by telling Bethany how much I loved her, that we were still within her five year window for a marriage proposal response, and I wanted to accept. I could not resist joking that I assumed she had not found the rich Bostonian who was good in bed.

Before she could speak, I went on to tell her I had only one more job assignment to complete before I was free of employment obligations. I wanted us to be married at that time. I thought we would be in a window of two to three months.

Then, from my coat pocket, I produced and offered her a diamond engagement ring. I had called Margo to get the ring size. Bethany had tears in her eyes as she held out her left hand for me to place the ring. We were in each others arms for only a brief moment before our flight was called.

On the plane – I had reserved first class – we took the usual offer of champagne. Now it was time for me to do some explaining.

I told her that the details of my work would have to always remain a secret. I would tell her, in strict confidence until my last assignment was complete, that I was working for the Central Intelligence Agency. At job completion, I would receive the promised letter of commendation that would specifically state that I had been in CIA employment since I left the army.

Bethany laughed that her high society acquaintances in Boston might spend hours trying to figure out the CIA involvement in the New York loan shark business.

At this point I got my first question. She wanted to know why we were going to Migerousy? The answer was that I wanted to see the island where my money was being deposited. I explained that my work was outside of regular CIA employment, so I was being paid from a special fund for such purposes. So that there would be no record, my monthly salary and the bonuses for each completed assignment, were sent to an account established for me with the Bank of Migerousy.

I also wanted to visit the island. All that I had read was good. It seemed to be a really nice place, good economy, almost no crime, ample entertainment, and a homogeneous, mostly European heritage, population. Bethany commented that it sounded like a place we could live.

After checking in our hotel, we took a taxi to the main office of the bank. I explained that I wanted to review the records of my account. After proper identification we were escorted to a private office where the account statements were delivered.

Bethany was shocked when she saw the balance well in excess of one million dollars. Then she saw that the account was joint. She was a co-owner. Her quick mind had her look through the account records to find the date she had been added as a joint owner.

It was about two years prior.

She turned to me with eyes flashing. "You did this without telling me two years ago. You have intended to marry me for all that time without letting me know. You are a real jerk! But a jerk I love very much, very, very much!"

With bank business complete, we went to a local watering hole to commence early cocktails before dinner. It was there that I reminded Bethany she had two news items for me.

The first was how the bonus week off came about. There was a prominent member of the United States House of Representatives from Boston that had been indicted for selling a stock holding after receiving inside confidential information from a Congressional Committee meeting. There was no doubt he sold his entire holding after learning in the meeting that the company was filing bankruptcy that would make his common stock worthless.

The Congressman was a client of Bethany's firm which did not take criminal defense matters. The firm sent him to a prominent lawyer skilled in criminal defense. Not wanting to be totally out of the representation of a major client, Bethany was assigned to perform any duties that might assist the criminal defense lawyer.

There was really nothing for her to do, but she decided to review the history of the bankrupting company from inception to the present. In reading news articles about the company, she came across one obscure opinion by a little known financial analyst that had been written about a month before the information came to the Congressional Committee. He speculated that the company was in a dire financial strain without much in the way of facts to support his opinion.

Bethany gave the article to the defense lawyer, telling him that the opinion had a lack of supporting data, and that a man as busy as the Congressman would have been highly unlikely to have read it. The defense lawyer smiled as he told her he could guarantee the opinion had been read.

The lawyer told the Congressman to lie and claim he had read the opinion, using it to decide to sell his stock before attending the committee hearing.

This defense, in the hands of a skilled defense lawyer, resulted in the Congressman being acquitted of the crime charged. The defense lawyer gave Bethany some credit, the Congressman was very pleased, and her reward was the week vacation. Bethany was the only one who thought anything was wrong with the deliberate lie under oath.

The other news involved my sister Anna. When she could not reach me, she had called Bethany. Her husband wanted a divorce and was asking Anna to agree to terms.

John and Anna had gone to his high school reunion in Wolftown, Michigan. At the festivities, John had reunited with his sweetheart of their junior and senior years at Wolftown High School. They had been secretly meeting at a motel between Wolftown and Monville since that time. Now, he was admitting to the relationship with an intention to divorce and remarry.

Anna was distraught and did not know what to do. She thought they were happy. She did not want a divorce. All of the lawyers in Monville were friends of John. She would have to go out of town to get legal counsel. John had said he would never agree to her taking their son away from Monville. While Anna had friends there, she did not want to live in a small town with John's new wife.

Bethany did not know what to do. Anna was so desperate. She decided to tell Anna I had a close friend that often had good ideas in solving problems. With Anna's permission, she called Nucci.

After hearing the facts from Bethany, Nucci got permission to call Anna. With Anna, it was agreed Nucci would travel to Monville to talk to John. There was a meeting of John and Nucci. Neither Anna or Bethany knew what transpired during the meeting, but John came home with an entirely new focus. He would stop seeing the old friend and would commit himself to saving the marriage.

I told Bethany I was sure I understood. Nucci was not only very smart, he was amazingly persuasive. John spent seven years in school in New York. Nucci's position with the mafia was not much of a secret. I did not know if the persuasion involved threats, logic or something else, but I was not surprised at what Nucci could accomplish.

I would call Anna as soon as our island trip was concluded.

CHAPTER FIFTY-SIX

As we were leaving the bar to prepare for dinner, I received a call from a Vice-President at the bank. Seeming to be a very pleasant man, he indicated that he had just learned we were on the island and would like to extend a last- minute invitation to dinner if we had not made plans. Having nothing in particular planned, Bethany and I accepted.

At the appointed time, Tony Tollison and wife, Melanie, arrived to take us to the Migerousy Country Club. It was a very nice facility with golf course, tennis courts, swimming pool, and a club house with a dining room and bar that would equal many such private clubs in large metropolitan areas.

Tony had arranged a table in the bar for before-dinner cocktails and small talk. Our conversation was easy. Tony became a transplant from London when he was hired by the island bank about twenty years before. He had spent five years with a London bank and was delighted to have an opportunity for island life.

Melanie had moved to Migerousy after a number of trips in her work as an airline stewardess. She was from a small town in the midwestern United States, living in Miami for her work, and found large-city life was not her choice. She had a Liberal Arts college degree which allowed her to find employment as a librarian.

Tony and Melanie met soon after both arrived, dated a few months, and had been married since. No children and none planned. Both were happy with their lives.

The dinner was exceptional. Of course, seafood was the specialty, and Tony was quite adept at wine selection. We ate, drank and talked for a couple of hours.

Melanie and Bethany really enjoyed each other. Melanie was insistent that she should take us over the island the next day. With nothing planned, we were pleased to have an island tour.

Migerousy was exceptionally clean, far beyond the norm for a medium- size city, and well-planned. The hotels and tourist attractions rimmed the coast line. The financial and business district was in the center with residential between that area and the coastal development. Schools and churches were primarily within the residential areas, as was the large library where Melanie worked.

Melanie was very convincing that we should consider this island as a home after our marriage. We would have a lot of considerations, family, friends, and employment, but this thought was not out of the realm of reason as our lives moved on.

We stayed one more day and night before the flight back to Boston. We had so much future to talk out. Living in Boston, living in New York, possibly trying small-town life, even Migerousy. Many issues, but a lot of love to solve them.

One thing was becoming apparent. Bethany did not like the idea of long-term employment with her law firm, even with the money she would earn as a partner. Her main problem was the monetary cheating of the clients, the over-billing by adding hours not actually worked. It was prevalent in the firm, known to most all, and generally considered simply the way that business was done. Bethany really felt it was criminal.

Added to this was that she really did not like Boston, at least the Boston society that was such a part of the lives of the partners in the firm. But then, she added she would live anywhere I decided would best fit our marriage and lives.

One very nice thing was that we had enough money to make time for decisions after the most important thing, getting married. I did suggest, and Bethany agreed, not to wear the ring or announce our engagement until after I completed my last assignment. I hoped this would be soon.

CHAPTER FIFTY-SEVEN

It was only a few days after the island trip until the call came from Contact Red. We were to meet to discuss the details of my last assignment.

As usual, I listened intently to the background information.

I was the one assassin with the CIA who was uniquely qualified for this assignment. It involved the Russians. Russians spies were, except for the Chinese, the most prevalent in the United States and possibly in the entire world. They would know every agent of the CIA involved in kills except, hopefully, for me. I was relatively new and had not had any agency connection except for Contact Red.

Kostas Ivanov was a Russian secret agent who traveled the world in the guise of a Russian television reporter for international affairs. As a news reporter, he was allowed entry into most countries without questions as to his purposes. He might be in London one day and Cairo the next.

Contact Red went on to tell me that the United States was far from the only country that carried out assassinations throughout the world. Russia was our equal, and Kostas Ivanov was one of their best at government-ordered murder without being caught. The CIA had confirmed that he had killed one of our agents in Lebanon. We suspected that he had also killed a Ukrainian who was working as a spy for our country.

My assignment was to kill Ivanov. This was to be my most dangerous assignment. Ivanov had years of experience. He would know how to protect himself. I would have to be certain in my planning so that I did not end up as the murder victim.

Then, there was the issue of secrecy of my identity as his killer. I must escape from the kill without being or becoming known. The Russians have a long history of revenge. They have spent months, or years, waiting for the right opportunity to murder anyone known to have acted against their government. Their list of victims included political dissidents, activists, traitors, spies, and certainly assassins for other countries.

Even if I could kill Ivanov, escape and return to

the United States, I would never be secure if the Russians learned that I was the murderer. History says they would track me for the rest of my life to find an opportunity for deadly revenge.

Contact Red was so concerned that he offered to allow me to pass on this assignment and complete my obligation in a future matter. He did not know how much I wanted to move to completion to be with Bethany for the remainder of my life. I would plan carefully and accept the risk.

CHAPTER FIFTY-EIGHT

For the Ivanov assignment, I would be given an identity as a tourist from Italy moving around the world for entertainment and history research after acquiring substantial money from a deceased relative. I would be furnished an Italian passport, normal other identification, and several credit cards with high limits.

It was obvious I could not carry weapons on international aircraft travel. Wherever I traveled, I would be contacted by a local CIA operative who would provide anything I might need from weapons to information.

I would commence my journey with a flight to London. Intelligence was that Ivanov had made a London hotel reservation to commence in two days. I would be there to start my search for opportunity.

Ivanov usually traveled with a male companion who had the appearance and equipment of a news cameraman.

British government was in the midst of several contentious matters of international interest. It would appear Ivanov would be in London to cover the news developments. CIA information was that he might be there to plan and possibly carry out an assassination. There was a newspaper journalist from Russia, now living in London and writing for the London Times, who was a major critic of the Russian President. Rumors were that the journalist, Anna Politkov, might have carried her criticism to heights that were no longer acceptable to the Russian government.

These rumors were soon confirmed. Anna had dinner with her daughter in a well-known restaurant just outside London. Both died within twenty-four hours. Modern medical expertise was able to determine that each had soup containing gelsemium, a rare plant found only in remote parts of China and loaded with toxins related to strychnine.

I learned an important lesson. Be in conflict with the Russians and they might kill you and your children.

I had learned from Contact Red that the Russians established their first laboratory for the manufacture of poisons, the Kamera, in the third decade of the twentieth century. Their goal was to develop odorless, tasteless, and colorless poisons that victims could not detect when ingesting and which would leave no trace. If a political enemy was poisoned, and the poison was detected during autopsy, it would be deleted from use. Leaving no trace was then most important. Today, however, modern medical science has greatly improved detection of cause of death, as was shown by the determination in the Politkov murder.

While denied by the Russians, the number of deaths by poison in recent years has much of the world believing the poison laboratory still exists. According to Boris Volodarsky, a former Russian military-intelligence agent who authored the book "The KGB Poison Factory", Kamara physicians calculate a potential victim's height, weight, and other information in order to select a poison. The optimal dose is one that will kill the selected target, leave no trace, and result in a determination of death by natural causes.

While Ivanov and his cameraman appeared active from a news standpoint in the Anna Politkov murder, it was not mentioned in the Russian news channels. They were soon on their way to Spain.

CHAPTER FIFTY-NINE

I would follow Ivanov to Madrid, the capital city of Spain. I would not stay in his hotel or even nearby. He was the elite assassin for the Russians with much more experience than me. If he saw my face, even if only as little as twice during these travels, his training in recognition might be enough to arouse suspicion. I wanted to be sure to remain the hunter. I did not want to become the hunted.

Even though the airport in Madrid, "Barajas", is huge with its three terminals for domestic and international travelers, I made certain not to be on the same flight.

My contact in Spain gave me the hotel and arrangements for Ivanov and his travel companion. Two separate rooms, not unusual for two males not worried about expense, but this time a possible break for me. Ivanov had a female guest, a most attractive young Russian girl. As my information was that he had a wife at home in Russia, he might be less careful than usual during the course of an affair.

For two days and nights, he and his purported cameraman attended newsworthy events in the city. In the evenings, he and the girlfriend ate at two of the high end restaurants, among the best in all of Spain. I often used binoculars as I observed from a significant distance.

My instincts were that Madrid was not the place where my opportunity would arise. When not watching my target, I made the best of this travel by seeing some of the city sites.

Madrid is located in the middle of the Iberian Peninsula. As the capital of Spain, it is seat of the Spanish government and residence of the Royal family of Spain.

Madrid is larger than Barcelona with a metropolitan area population of more than three million. It has, of course, the Spanish natives, the "madrilenos", but the population is enhanced by an influx of people from other countries, especially from Latin America.

Traffic is heavy in the city with driving by visitors not recommended. Ivanov traveled by automobile with a hired local driver, while I used the metro, locally know as "the tube". I also did a lot of walking. Interesting sites abound in Madrid. It would have been educational to spend time as a true tourist, but I had to remain focused on my purpose.

I did have an incident. Madrid has a reputation for low crime with an exception for pick-pockets and bag thieves who are everywhere. As I was walking along a street with dim lighting, a young man bumped into me. He was an obvious pick-pocket, but I was prepared with my wallet and documents protected in zipped pockets.

The young men followed me closely, pushing me into a narrow alley. He showed a switch-blade knife while demanding my money and cell phone. It only took a second for me to send him unconscious to the alley floor. In his pockets were three wallets and one cell phone. I took these and the knife to deposit in a mail drop which I assumed would get the items to the local police.

The next morning Ivanov and the other man left on an airliner bound for Russia. His young female friend stayed in the Madrid hotel room. This seemed strange, but was clarified that evening.

The female friend was in the hotel bar at five o'clock for several drinks before leaving to dine alone at one of the most expensive restaurants. My local contact sat in a corner of the bar and listened to this very talkative female. Her constant conversation with the bartender revealed her name to be Raisa Volkov. She was to stay in Madrid for three more days before flying to Amsterdam to meet her boyfriend. He had gone back to Russia to get a divorce and would join her for a week in the Netherlands in celebration of his freedom from a wife of a dozen years.

My confusion and curiosity about the divorce was clarified that night by my contact. It seems that Russia has a quite simple procedure for dissolution of a marriage. If the parties are willing to apply for the divorce together, their application is made in a registry office. Then, a month later, the registry gives a specific date the paper confirming the divorce can be collected. If one or both appears to collect the paper, the divorce is officially acknowledged. If no one comes, the divorce process is ended and the couple remains married.

Assuming no children, the law provides everything purchased during the marriage is equally divided. Personal belongings, gifts and inheritances are not subject to the division.

If the parties do not agree to apply together, the divorce must be commenced in court. But, as the law is so specific, it is rare to spend large amounts on a court proceeding when the outcome is virtually certain. Even with children, the amount of support is very specific.

Russia has a high rate of divorce which is likely attributed to the ease of the process with small expense.

I decided to leave Madrid to proceed to Amsterdam the next morning. A few days head start would give me time to make plans. This seemed like a most opportune time to take out Ivanov while he was involved in the romance with Raisa.

CHAPTER SIXTY

Amsterdam has got to be one of the most interesting cities in the world. I had several days to visit famous sites that would be filled with tourists. I would carefully observe, and would try to figure the most likely places that would be visited by the couple, to find a location where the assassination could take place.

Ivanov, with his new love, would not likely be as careful as he would be under different circumstances. Though he might be easy to kill, the bigger problem could be my escape without detection. I would require much direction from my CIA contact in this Dutch city. He was already working. I was informed of the hotel reservations and several tours that had been booked.

Any visitor must take in the Red Light District. This several blocks is home to bars that feature drugs as well as alcohol. But the main attraction is the prostitutes. They occupy glass-front rooms in buildings lining the streets. If open for business, the girl will be standing behind the glass dressed (or not dressed) to attract a customer. The customer knocks on the door and, should a deal be made, enters the room which has a bed. The curtain is pulled over the glass before the sexual pleasure begins. The purchase may be for oral sex, intercourse, or both, but with a requirement for a condom to be used. After the fifteen or twenty minutes involved, the customer leaves, the curtain is opened, and the girl is again soliciting in the window.

I could be certain the couple would take in this attraction. With all of the people along the streets, an opportunity to kill Ivanov would be likely. I just could not figure any route of escape, so I moved on to other attractions.

Ivanov had a reservation to visit the Anne Frank house. The building is located on the Prinsengracht canal in central Amsterdam. This museum is dedicated to the Jewish wartime diarist.

During World War II, Anne Frank, then a child, hid in rooms at the rear of the canal house with her family and four other people, all Jews, in an attempt to avoid the Nazi persecution. After a couple of years, some person still unknown, informed the Germans. All were taken to be exterminated in the massive Nazi murders of Jews.

The Anne Frank story would have most likely never have been publicly known except for her extensive diary which was found and published after the war.

The museum preserves the hiding place, has an exhibition on the life of Anne Frank, and additional space covering persecution and discrimination in many forms.

I enjoyed my visit to the Anne Frank museum, but it had no potential for my plan.

There were two famous artists whose paintings are preserved in major museums that Ivanov and friend would surely visit. These are the Rijksmuseum and the Van Gogh Museum. Even with my limited knowledge of matters of art, I was well aware of Vincent Van Gogh. I required education
as to Rijks.

A young man studying art in Amsterdam heard my inquiry and volunteered to tell me all about Rijks. I would not be rude by interrupting his spiel of information which far exceeded all I wanted to know.

A couple of hundred years before Van Gogh, there was another Dutch painter, Rembrandt van Rijn, known in modern times simply as Rembrandt. Maybe equally famous with Van Gogh, his paintings are a primary feature of the Rijksmuseum.

My art student suggested I should see the artwork known as the "Jewish Bride". This portrait of a male and female was long ago thought to be of a just-married Jewish couple. Although that thought was later found to be incorrect, the name stayed with one of Rembrandt's best-known works.

The most prominently displayed and most famous painting in the Rijks is a 1642 work by Rembrandt. The long original title was "Militia Company of District II under the Command of Captain Frans Banning Cocq." It became also known as "The Shooting Company of Frans Banning Cocq and Willem van Ruytenburch". I could have just been told that it is commonly referred to as "The Night Watch".

"The Night Watch" is famous for its colossal size,

almost twelve feet by fifteen feet, the dramatic use of light and shadow, and the perception of motion of the military group.

I thanked the young man before leaving to view the two paintings he had described in such detail. I was not disappointed as they are both magnificent even to my totally untrained eyes.

When I relocated to the Van Gogh museum, I was fortunate to find a guide
who was not occupied. Like my Rembrandt art student, he was well- informed and anxious to lay out his knowledge in much detail.

Though Van Gogh may be the most famous painter in all of history, his life was a financial and personal disaster. It is commonly believed that, of his hundreds of paintings, only a small portion was sold during his life. He was a mentally ill genius who was supported by his brother Theo.

When Van Gogh died in 1890, his work became the possession of Theo. Theo died shortly thereafter leaving the collection to his widow, Johanna van Gogh-Bonger. Johanna sold many of the paintings, but maintained a private collection of the works.

This private collection was inherited by her son Vincent Willem van Gogh in 1925. It was eventually transferred to the state- sponsored Vincent van Gogh Foundation and finally came to rest in the Van Gogh Museum.

The museum guide had a few interesting follow-up stories to the establishment of the Van Gogh Museum.

In 1991, twenty paintings were stolen from the museum, including an early work "The Potato Eaters". The artwork was recovered in less than an hour, but with three of the works sustaining damage in the theft.

In 2002, two more paintings, "Congregation Leaving the Reformed Church in Nuenen" and "View of the Sea at Scheveningen" were stolen. The criminals were found and convicted, but the art was not recovered. Some years later the paintings were found in Naples, Italy having at time-of- recovery an estimated value of thirty million dollars.

I was interested enough to spend a couple of hours in the museum. One could see Van Gogh as, four years prior to his death, he painted a self-portrait showing his red hair and beard with a pipe in his mouth.

Between Rembrandt and Van Gogh, I had an educational experience that could be of value if I needed cocktail conversation with some of Bethany's high-society law office partners. Otherwise, I was no closer to finding the right place to carry out my assignment.

CHAPTER SIXTY-ONE

Finally, my local CIA operative had some information that could solve my problem. He had learned that Ivanov and Raisa had planned two different day trips, one to Volendam and the other to Simonehoeve, a popular attraction in the village of Katwoude, which is very near, actually almost in, Volendam.

In the countryside villages outside of Amsterdam, I should be able to locate a place for the kill and a route of escape. I would rent a car tomorrow to travel to both areas. I had learned that only two of twelve provinces comprising the Netherlands were technically known as Holland, although sometimes Holland is used as a name for all of the Netherlands. Where I would go is often known as Old Holland and the people as Dutch.

I found Simonehoeve to be quite a tourist attraction. If one bought the experience, upon arrival, they would be transformed into a real Dutchman or woman, dressed in traditional Dutch costume. A pair of wooden shoes would be available on request.

There would be a guided tour of the cheesefarm and the clog shoe factory. The tour package included the tasting of cheeses, biscuits and fruitwine. Of course, photographs and souvenirs could be purchased.

This was all very interesting, but offered none of the opportunity that I needed. I drove the short distance on to Volendam.

I found that Volendam is known as a fishing village that has typical authentic little houses. Because of this, walking around through the old neighborhoods is the popular way of discovery. Throughout the Dijk or the Doolhof, a labyrinth of lanes, there are old fishermen's houses that have appealed to painters and artists for centuries.

In the Palingsound (eel sound) Museum, there is the pop music known throughout the area. Paling is for eel in the Dutch language and references the eels making their sounds. In the same building at the harbor, you will find the Smit Bokkum eel smokehouse which features tours showing how eel has been smoked in centuries-old tradition.

Following a tour, the in-house restaurant serves tasty eel dishes.

Then there is the Volendams Museum where the typical costume of the fishing village is on display. Also displayed are ship's models, paintings, and other art works. There are rooms decorated and arranged as they would have been in the last century. Among the rooms is a curious collection that belonged to a local man who decorated the walls of his actual room with mosaics made from eleven million cigar bands.

I thought that the man must have been a weird collector of every cigar band he could find as smoking eleven million cigars, even for a chain smoker, would be a little much for one lifetime.

The harbor area also included the Wooden Shoe Factory where the Dutch wooden shoes, known as klompen, are made, and the Cheese Factory Volendam which features cheeses made in the traditional production methods. Cheese could be purchased and also wooden shoes which were said to be comfortable to wear in your home garden.

Experience Volendam, using modern technology,

is another attraction which shows Dutch living quarters from the early twentieth century in a holographic display, and a stormy ship voyage from the same period in a virtual reality film.

I had found my location. Volendam seemed to be just what I needed. It was a small, somewhat crowed area, where walking around to the number of sites was standard. Ivanov and Raisa could be easily followed. I could arrange to kill him, blend into the confusion, and simply walk away to a meeting place to leave the village with my contact. The method of the murder would have to be considered as would arrangement to obtain the weapon.

My CIA contact met with me in my hotel room that night. I thought we would be discussing potential weapons to use. I was quickly informed that had already been decided. This murder was too important and too delicate for the details to be left only to me. It became obvious that Washington was in control of the operation.

I would carry a mini folded, but fake, umbrella that was nine inches in length. Inside the fake umbrella was an eight inch long aluminum tube. Upon pointing the umbrella and pulling the trigger in the handle, a colorless, odorless poison carefully sealed in a thin capsule would be shot out of the hermetically sealed aluminum tube into my victims face. This capsule, which can be fired from twenty-four inches, would produce almost instant death. The deadly vapors are breathed into the lungs. Arteries that carry blood to the brain are paralyzed instantly. Within seconds, the victim begins to die. Within minutes, all traces of the poisonous vapor disappear. If there is a subsequent autopsy, there will be no evidence of the poison. The cause of death would probably be listed as a heart attack.

While I had no problem using this weapon, I did mention to my contact that I had been told that the United States no longer possessed poisons such as we would be using. The answer was that there were certain secrets within the CIA, and other agencies protecting our country, that I would be well served by not knowing.

I would wear a disguise when I returned to Volendam. My contact had a suitcase of wigs, mustaches, and glasses for me to try. The selection was a gray wig, matching mustache, and large dark glasses. The clothes I would wear were typical for tourists. Even though cameras are everywhere tourists carry cell-phones, I was comfortable that my appearance would be very concealed even if compared to my looks earlier that day in the village.

Ivanov was to visit Volendam in two days. I had watched the weather projections carefully. It appeared there was no chance of weather that might cancel a tourist day. I was very nervous as I waited for the big day.

I spent my time thinking of Bethany. If I could just get by this assignment
without any screw up, all of my life with her was ahead. I so wanted to call her, but knew I had to wait. Oh well, I could drink wine and dream of her while I waited.

CHAPTER SIXTY-TWO

My big day had arrived. I showered, put on my tourist clothes, and carefully put my disguise in place, spending an inordinate amount of time in front of a mirror. A teenage girl dressing for her first prom might have spent less.

I met my contact at his car. He would park just outside the village and wait for me. We had no conversation as he drove from Amsterdam to Volendam except he asked if I had my weapon. I wore a tourist backpack that contained the deadly umbrella.

I was pleased that the village was filled with tourists. Even more so when I spotted Ivanov and his girlfriend. My plan was simple. I would carry the umbrella in my hand as I followed my target at a distance. After what seemed to be a very long time, I saw him headed for a restroom. Following him in, I noticed one man in a closed stall and only Ivanov at a urinal. I moved to his side. As he looked over toward me, I fired my weapon.

He managed three words, "what the fuck...", before falling to the floor. I was out the door, leaving the man on the toilet to find a dead man.

I walked slowly so as not to draw attention. It was about a minute before I heard a man yelling for help. A short time after, there was a women screaming that was surely Raisa. By that time, I was almost to the waiting car.

We drove slowly back to Amsterdam. My contact took my disguise and the umbrella. I was to stay in my hotel for two days so as not to be noticed leaving the city immediately after the death.

From Amsterdam, I was to travel by train to Belgium, continuing my tourist activities for three more days until a flight from Brussels to Rome. After two days in Rome, I would finally get to go home.

I had been instructed not to call Bethany until I was back in New York. These precautions were because the Russians were very suspicious. Though there would be no evidence that the death was not natural, they would always question if the United States could have been involved.

Back in New York, I reported to Contact Red. Our intelligence was that the Russians were trying to trace every American that had been in the Netherlands at the time of Ivanov's death. Since my passport and identification was fake, I had traveled as an Italian citizen with no United States connection. I should be clear.

Contact Red congratulated me on the successful completion of my final assignment. My pay had been deposited in my island account and my letter of completion of service from the CIA would be in the mail.

Now I could call Bethany.

CHAPTER SIXTY-THREE

When Bethany answered her phone, I had a feeling for which I could find no words. I simply thought it is real. I am just in love with her.

I could tell her my job was completed. No more secret travel, no more being apart for months at a time. It was time to plan a forever life together. It was Friday. I could be in Boston at her apartment when she got home from work that afternoon.

My sassy love told me she could put off the four or five men wanting to get in her pants over the weekend, so we had a date. I would bring wine, we would order pizza, and our new life together would commence.

Bethany left work early, arriving shortly after me. There was a lot of hugging, kissing, and a trip to her bedroom. We then cuddled on her sofa, opened wine, and commenced a night of talk of our future. Before leaving the bedroom, she opened a drawer to take out the engagement ring I had given her. She put the ring on, telling me I had better be serious about marriage as the ring was never coming off her finger.

Bethany made clear that she would work into her partnership with the law firm if the money she would earn was important. I could tell, however, she really did not like the firm and, most probably, would not choose to live in Boston. I reminded her we had well over one million dollars in our island bank account in Migerousy. While this money would not last a life-time, it was certainly enough that we would not be pressed to make quick decisions about our future.

After our great weekend, on Monday, Bethany told her senior partner she was leaving. There was a quick senior partners meeting. Bethany was the best of all the upcoming associates. They made a dual proposal. If she stayed, they would waive the five year requirement to immediately make her a junior partner. If she still wanted to leave, they offered a one year leave of absence, no pay, but a continuation of her medical insurance, during which time she could return as a junior partner. The leave had no downside, so she accepted, and we moved on with plans.

What to do about a wedding required some thought. My only relatives were my sister and her family. Bethany had her family who would want to host a wedding, but would be under a financial strain to do so. The best solution might be to marry and then inform the families.

I had an idea. We needed to invest some of our money in the bank account. We could go to Migerousy and call on Tony at the bank for some financial advice on investing money. A little island time would clear our heads on moving forward to marry.

Upon arriving in Migerousy, we rented a condo on the beach. The weather was warm and beautiful.

Tony seemed glad to hear from us and arranged an afternoon appointment at the bank. Bethany called Melanie to extend an invitation for us to take them to dinner. Melanie was insistent that we would have an informal dinner at their home. Tony would grill burgers in their back yard after cocktails. We would then take a walk so that we could see the neighborhood. It was obvious Melanie thought she and Bethany could be good friends. And we should consider living on the island.

The meeting at the bank was productive. Tony was a knowledgeable investment adviser. He was also good on an outdoor grill. We had a most pleasant evening at their home. The neighborhood was even nicer than expected. Melanie was quick to point out that there was one small house listed for sale that would just fit a couple of newlyweds.

After a few days, our decisions were made. We bought the house near Tony and Melanie. After marriage, we would live the island life for one year during which we would figure out the future. Tony wanted Bethany to interview for a position as an in-house lawyer for the bank. I would have time to search out prospects for some work with my limited qualifications.

The promised letter from the Director of the CIA had arrived just before we left for the island. The letter was exactly according to the agreement. It stated that I had left army service as a member of the special forces to join the CIA in a special capacity of secret operations which I had completed in an outstanding manner worthy of commendation.

The timing of movement from military service directly to the CIA cleared my ugly past in the loan shark business. The letter would be my entry into respectable business.

We decided to get married in New York just as my sister had done. Bethany called Margo to make the arrangement and to be our witness in the civil ceremony.

We took a flight to the big city, completed our marriage, and left the municipal building with marriage certificate in hand. As we reached the street, Nucci and Rosa appeared. Margo swore she did not tell Nucci, and I believed her. He had a way of always knowing everything that was going on.

There was a nice wedding gift from Nucci and Rosa, and a less expensive, but equally nice, gift from Margo.

We left New York for a few days with my sister and family, then traveled on for a week with Bethany's family. I believed that all were pleased we had taken the route away from a formal wedding.

We left the midwest on a flight to Miami and on to our new island home. Upon arrival, Bethany was informed she had been selected for the bank lawyer position to start work immediately.

I did not like that she would be working while I was not employed. This quickly changed. I had given Tony a copy of my letter from the CIA. He had learned of a local company that was interested in hiring a head of company security. The owner was so impressed with my military and CIA record that I was almost hired before an interview.

We were husband and wife, both with jobs, and living in a new home that we had already paid for. We were on a beautiful island. We were in love and life could not be better.

CHAPTER SIXTY-FOUR

On our flight back to the island, Bethany for the first time asked some questions about the work I had done for the CIA. I explained, and she accepted, that I could only say I had traveled and would tell her some of the places I had been. Otherwise, I was bound to secrecy.

In fact, I could and did tell Bethany I had been warned there are stiff legal penalties for discussing work or experiences with this government agency. One in violation could be taken into custody without a warrant, held indefinitely without bond procedure, and then brought to a secret trial. This was enough explanation for my lawyer wife. Her questions would not be asked again regardless of curiosity.

Social life on our island was very good. Tony and Melanie immediately became close friends. They introduced us to all of their many friends and, importantly, had the appropriate committee extend a membership in the country club which we promptly accepted.

My job had no specific hours. I was in charge of five employees who covered three eight hour shifts six days per week. I would train any new employee and work out all scheduling of vacations and absences. The owner needed to have a person to be in charge, but the salary I was being paid was well above market for someone in my capacity. I thought my business owner was making so much money that my salary was meaningless. He seemed to like having someone on board with my military/CIA record. In conversation, I could tell he was impressed by the secrecy involved.

Bethany had one other lawyer and a paralegal in her department at the bank. Her hours were eight to four-thirty Monday through Friday. Nothing like the seventy to eighty hours per week required in Boston. Time off was very liberal, and she had full insurance benefits with a retirement plan. While certainly not being paid like a major firm partner, she was well above someone like Margo in New York.

After paying for the house from the CIA money which Tony now had well invested, we were together making more than we would spend living the good life.

In social conversation, Bethany joked with Tony that her hours in Boston probably exceeded the weekly hours of both lawyers at the bank. He replied that she would find island life laid back and happy without the stress of the big city. This was so true.

Neither of us had ever been fishing. A group of our new friends extended an invitation to go on a charter boat trip to an offshore reef where we would fish for red snapper. Early on a Saturday morning, the group left for the reef. They explained that the fish would be near the bottom about one hundred feet down. The hooks were baited and we were had rods to drop the bait to the bottom. There was an almost immediate tug of a fish on the line. Now the hard part. A heavy fish had to be brought to the surface by many hard turns of the reel.

Often the size of the fish was just under the legal limit. The undersized had to be thrown back into the water, supposedly to live. In reality the fish was an easy meal for the waiting dolphins.

Bethany and I had been positioned on the starboard side near the front of the boat with a deckhand to bait our hooks and place any fish of adequate size in ice. After about two hours, we were exhausted and asked for a break. At that point, our friends confessed we were the subject of a novice fisherman's initiation. Where we were placed, we did not notice that the others had electric reels that brought the fish to the surface with no effort. After a lot of laughs, the heavy drinking for the remainder of the trip was in full swing.

Back in port, the crew cleaned the fish. We were given an ample quantity with instructions as to cooking it on the grill. It would take several tries to become grill-proficient.

Like fishing, neither of us had played tennis, a game that was big on the island. The country club had a tennis professional who gave lessons. Bethany and I both signed up. I found that my athletic ability was suited for this game. Within a couple of months, with lessons and a lot of practice, I could compete against all but the best players in the club. Tony had been playing for years, and we had a good competitive competition that was a lot of fun.

Bethany did not have my athletic ability, but she was competitive. There was a large group of women playing tennis at the club, so she could always have a game. This led to more friendships. We were beginning to feel like this island was really our home.

CHAPTER SIXTY-FIVE

The other lawyer with Bethany at the bank resigned to marry a man she had met at a bank lawyers convention in Tennessee. Tony assigned Bethany the duty of finding a replacement.

Tony had been promoted to Executive Vice-President and would soon succeed the President when he retired in a few months.

He kidded Bethany that she should not prove that she could handle the work of both positions. She well could have. Tony worked fairly hard himself, but was a believer that an island-time pace was best for most workers on Migerousy. Bethany was to be promoted to senior attorney with a raise in salary. The lawyer she would hire would take her present position and salary. Any sincere applicant would be flown to the island for an interview.

I was the one who suggested that Margo might have an interest. She agreed to come down, visit, take a look at our island, and consider the job change.

We had a grand time. Margo was the same as always. We ate, drank, and recalled old times. I would never mention, but I had thought over the years about what would have happened if Nucci had selected Bethany, and not Margo, as his evening companion on the first occasion of their agreement. I am sure I would have enjoyed Margo, but she would not have been the love of my life.

After some consideration, Margo decided she was a big city person, and would forgo the island life. I thought she was making the best decision for her personal satisfaction.

Before she left, she told Bethany that she was no longer going out with Nuccci. We were pleased to hear that he had decided Rosa deserved better in their senior years and would no longer step outside the marriage. While Margo had enjoyed the occasional affair, she was very happy for Rosa. She was still dating a number of single men, avoiding those married, and enjoying the unmarried life.

There was an aspect of island life we had not tried. Snorkeling. I had not learned to swim until required to do so in the military. My part of New York was not noted for swimming facilities.

Bethany had learned during her childhood.

There was an old shipwreck not far offshore where fishing was prohibited in favor of snorkeling and diving. Boats left on the half-hour to go out to the site. All had rental equipment. A quick lesson on snorkeling and we were in the water. The water was clear and clean. The fish, in all sizes and colors, were beautiful. We swam together, holding hands, enjoying our new experience. That is, until we noticed a number of rather large fish with vicious-looking teeth. This was our first experience with barracuda.

While the others in the water did not seem disturbed, we were totally bluffed out. We swam swiftly back to our boat to await the return home. We would stay out of water which was not very close to shore.

Bethany did find and hire another lawyer for the bank, a nice, attractive, young woman that had just graduated from law school in Virginia. She was a native of Migerousy who was delighted to find a position in her home community.

My tennis game was becoming strong for the

short time I had spent in learning and play. Bethany was on a women's tennis ladder which afforded much fun. For the nominal cost, the country club was an important part of our happy life.

Likewise, our friendship with Tony and Melanie was good. We would drink and dine together at least twice each week in addition to playing tennis. While Tony and I enjoyed competition, the girls were happy with fun and exercise, often followed by cocktails and food.

The new lawyer at her bank was doing well and could handle most matters without help. Bethany could take a week off and wanted to visit her parents. I was involved in some job training and could not leave at that time. This would be the first time we had been apart since our marriage.

I would take Bethany to the airport, but only after we were almost late for the flight because we decided on last-minute sex before her trip. We had been married for some time, but often acted like the honeymoon was still a part of our marriage. Lovers who were deeply in love.

We could not know how our lives were about to change.

CHAPTER SIXTY-SIX

While Bethany was away, I was invited to join Tony and Melanie for dinner at the country club. Arriving a little early, I sat at the bar to have a drink while I waited.

The bartender was a young girl I had not seen before. She told me this was her first day, but that she was experienced at a couple of bars in Miami before moving to this island. When I was hesitating over a drink to order, she suggested I should try her best drink, a salty dog. While this was not a choice I would have made, I thought to please a new club employee and accept the suggestion. The drink was adequate except for what I thought was an excess of salt.

Tony and Melanie arrived on time. I changed to my favorite red wine following the salty dog. The conversation was good, the food was excellent, and the only fault with the evening was that I went home to a house without Bethany for the first time since our marriage. We did talk on the phone. She was enjoying the visit to her family.

The next morning I was not feeling well. I had nothing important at work so I decided to lay around at home. Later in the day, after a light lunch, I did vomit, but then felt somewhat better. When we talked that night, I did not tell Bethany I could be sick as I did not want her to worry while with the family.

The next morning, I felt as if I had might have gotten a case of flu. It was then that I received a cell phone call from a woman who said Contact Red must speak to me on an emergency basis. He came on the phone with news that was disturbing. Not just disturbing, maybe for the first time I could recall, making me fearful.

I was told there was a long-time employee at his section of the CIA, Mary Donald, a female secretary, who had worked in this same office for near forty years. She had never married, had no family or known friends, and her entire life was around her work. She was totally trusted.

Unknown to anyone at the CIA, she had somehow discovered casino slot machine gambling. Every weekend, and for all of her vacation and days off, she was in a casino playing the slots. Her addiction led to losses she could not afford. All of her savings was gone, her credit cards maxed out, her home fully mortgaged, and her unsecured bank loan limit exhausted. It was bankruptcy time in her life.

It was the Russians who knew about Mary's activity and dire financial condition. They still believed Ivanov had been assassinated by United States agents. Mary was their chance for information. She was offered all of her lost money for the name of any CIA operative in Amsterdam at the time of Ivanov's death. She gave up my name for the money.

When I told Contact Red I had been feeling bad, he asked about any unusual food or drink, I mentioned the salty dog. He said that salt was often used to disguise any taste from poisons. A military plane would be at the airport in a few hours to take me to a naval hospital that had a unit specializing in poison assessment and treating. They had physicians studying the poisons used by governments around the world and trying to determine the best treatments.

Waiting at the airport, I called the country club.

The salty dog bartender had left at the end of her one shift, had not returned the next day, and had left no message. I then knew the Russians had gotten me. I just did not know how bad it was.

By the time I reached the hospital, I was unable to eat and breathing had become difficult. After a few tests, the doctors had determined that I had been given Polonium-210, a radioactive isotope from uranium that had actually been discovered in the late nineteenth century by Marie and Pierre Curie.

In small doses, there was some possibility of a cure over a month or more. For a large dose, there is no cure. I had been given such a high dose that my death was inevitable. If fact, I was isolated from all except necessary medical staff as my body was actually radioactive.

A military plane had been sent for Bethany. She was in the hospital, but could not come to my special room designed for radioactive trauma. She was nearly hysterical.

Contact Red told Bethany all that he could under the circumstances. He explained that I had performed a service that took down a significant spy operation by a foreign government. They had managed to discover my identity and had poisoned me in retaliation.

Bethany tried to talk to me over the waiting area to room communications. She was so upset little could be said over her crying. She was joined at the hospital by Margo and Nucci who were able to provide some comfort.

My condition was worse by the hour. Over the next several days, I could feel that I would soon die. The medical staff had done everything possible.

The following morning was scheduled for a Catholic priest visit to be followed by Bethany being allowed in my room for thirty minutes. I would refuse to die this night. All that was left for me was to see Bethany.

I had nausea all through that night and found my hair was beginning to fall out. My throat had swollen to a point that I could not drink fluid. There was pain throughout my body. Speaking was difficult. The Russians did not only want to kill me, they wanted me to suffer. They had done a damn good job.

In the morning, a Catholic priest, who was a naval officer, administered the last rites. As soon as he was finished, Bethany was allowed into my room. She tried to speak, but was unable to get words out through her flood of tears.

I tried to say how much I loved her. A few words came out through my swollen throat.

Bethany climbed into bed with me, holding me and crying throughout the entire time allowed. She was unable to speak through the tears. When the nurse came for her, she managed to gain enough control to say she would always love me. **Then she was gone!**

I am growing weaker by the hour. It is all I can do to write my final words before I die. My Catholic religion says earthly death is not the end, but there is another, better life. I will soon know. If there is more, perhaps I will meet you there.

Whatever may be, I hope you have enjoyed reading my story – **Goodbye!**

the end